STAY IN YOUR LAYNE

Alliances are broken and hearts stolen.

BROKEN ALLIANCES SERIES
BOOK 1

SADIE WINCHESTER

For all those who never thought they could:

Life is short. Do the thing.

OFFICIAL PLAYLIST

Blow (ft. Spencer Charnas) - Eva Under Fire

Breathe Underwater - Bullet For My Valentine

Coming Undone - Korn

Contemptress (ft. Maria Brink) - Motionless In White

Harder To Breathe - Letdown.

Just Pretend - Bad Omens

Little Fight Left - Tommee Profitt, Fleurie, Jung Youth

Love the Way You Hate Me - Like A Storm

One For The Money - Escape The Fate

Popular Monster - Falling In Reverse

Save Yourself - My Darkest Days

Snuff - Slipknot

Take Me Back To Eden - Sleep Token

THE DEATH OF PEACE OF MIND - Bad Omens

The Very Last Time - Bullet For My Valentine

Voices In My Head - Falling In Reverse

When The Darkness Comes - Jeris Johnson

You're Going Down - Sick Puppies

Your Betrayal - Bullet For My Valentine

The official playlist can be found on Spotify.

(Tap "Search" in the Spotify app, tap the camera icon, scan and go!)

CONTENT & TRIGGER WARNINGS

This book ends on a cliffhanger. Contains adult content for 18+ readers only. Included, but not limited to, is a list of content/trigger warnings below:

Abduction, Alcohol, Blood/Gore, Hospitalization (brief), Masturbation, Perceived Cheating / OWD, Possessive Behavior, Profanity, Sexually Explicit Scenes, Toxic Relationships, and Violence (Bombs, Murder, etc.).

Disclaimers: There may be light, thematic BDSM elements within the story, and should not be construed as representative of a BDSM lifestyle and/or dynamic.

Your mental health matters.

Please visit SadieWinchester.com or email SadieWinchesterAuthor@gmail.com with any questions regarding content/trigger warnings.

CHAPTER ONE

Three years ago

She had been away from home for the past four years. Had it been Layne's choice? Hell the fuck no. She would have preferred to stay in the Upper East Side, where she had been born and raised in New York.

According to her father, going to school for an education and degree was far more valuable than deep diving into the family business. Insert Layne's aggressive eye roll here. However, she had a solid hunch that he had sent her away to get her off his back about getting more heavily involved in his business dealings of the organized crime persuasion.

You see, her family was at the pinnacle of power in the city's criminal underworld, and her father sat at the top of his organization as the kingpin.

Another reason to send her away to the other side of the country? So she would stop picking fights and inserting herself into legitimately dangerous situations.

Layne couldn't help herself. She had always had an attitude the size of the Hudson, and an even bigger right hook. Just ask Rob Holmes, her first (ex) boyfriend from when she was in the tenth grade. Nothing topped getting your clock rung by a girl in front of the entire gym class.

Living out on the West Coast at UCLA for the last four years didn't change any of those pesky personality traits. The only thing going out west got her was an expensive piece of paper and time to polish her fighting technique with a few high-end trainers. Daddy didn't even realize what his money was paying for. The one thing she didn't come home with? A tan. Damn her Irish genetics.

Most people knew her father as Scott O'Reilly—Scotty to his closest confidants. When questions were asked about the details of the family business? It was always don't ask, don't tell. The criminal underworld they operated in was a carefully crafted web of a few legitimate business transactions, under-the-table negotiations, and outright violence and intimidation tactics.

Her dad took pride in his heritage, having been born in a small town just south of Limerick, his mother and father moved themselves over to the U.S. when he was a wee lad of just two years old. Any traces of an accent were nonexistent, but the Irish tricolor ran through every fiber of his being.

The hired associates who took orders from Mr. O'Reilly were part of a local network of men of mostly Irish-Catholic descent throughout the footprint of Manhattan. Most of them were well-versed in the sketched-out operations within the shadows of the underworld. There was no sense in hiring rebellious kids who were looking to make a quick buck and potentially get a stint behind bars due to their irresponsible fuckups.

Any women that were part of the network of employees merely had the archaic supporting role of either popping out all the babies or being the friendly entertainment for all those hardworking men her father employed.

From a young age, Layne knew that she was not like the other ladies she saw coming and going from O'Reilly Manor at all hours of the night. By contrast, there was her mother who embodied the epitome of the finest maternal attributes and had played the role of a perfectly doting wife and homemaker. Shannon O'Reilly had embraced her position within the family structure, invested in maintaining the public-facing image of a well-adjusted family unit.

Iron-willed, stubborn women looking to make waves were not welcome in this particular enterprise.

As for little Miss Layne O'Reilly? She had wanted to be involved in business operations for as long as she could recall. However, her father had always discouraged her or outright prayed she'd grow out of such a silly aspiration. Scott insisted on telling her that a beautiful young lady need not be worried about these sorts of matters. Insert yet another heavily used eye roll here.

Instead, when it came to business, her father favored his youngest child, Liam, who was only eleven months younger than Layne. Liam was going to be the big man in charge one day, and it showed in the opportunities he was given as a means to get his hands dirty.

Meanwhile, Layne was only given almost anything and everything an uptown girl could have asked for. Yet, Liam was going to be handed the O'Reilly legacy. It pissed her off.

The driver pulled up in front of the multi-million dollar townhome that belonged to the O'Reilly family—O'Reilly Manor as it was frequently referred to. She had grown up inside of this house with some fond and some not-so-fond memories.

When the driver promptly rounded the Escalade and opened the door for her, Layne tossed her phone back into her jacket pocket and stepped out onto the sidewalk.

"Thanks, Artie." She offered him a polite smile as she stood right outside the expansive residence, taking in the view and mentally preparing for yet another drawn-out conversation about her future and role in this family. Artie gave a nod of his head and stood there at full attention, in the event she needed anything further from him.

Drawing one more deep breath, she gathered a little more courage inside of her to take the first step. Confidence was going to be key here.

Layne approached the stone steps that led up to two wrought iron gated doors protectively situated ahead of the front door, and let herself through both entranceways into the interior of the excessively opulent residence. Everything was as she recalled it; polished floors, sparkling chandeliers, high-end artwork, and cold. It was not physically cold, but nothing inside the house made it feel like a home. Not anymore anyway. Even burning a damn Yankee Candle would have helped.

She had arrived wearing a dark pair of blue jeans and a cream-colored blouse under a fitted cargo-styled jacket.

Layne's favorite pair of heeled boots gave the ensemble a pop of her grittier personality. Her lengthy locks of dark chestnut hair were gently pulled back away from her face into a simplistic ponytail. The depths of her stunning emerald eyes scanned the foyer for any signs of activity. That's when she heard it.

"I don't give a damn! You go back and tell that mother-fucker that if there is so much as a whisper about his people stepping foot in my territory, I will personally deliver each one back piece-by-piece in shoeboxes!" The familiar thunderous male voice boomed from down the hall where a mahogany door had been left ajar. There was a pause, followed by some quieter voices discussing something or other.

Layne approached, keeping her ears open to see if she could garner additional context on what her father had been shouting about. Right as she got to the door to the office, it swung open as Mick, her father's second in command, was on his way out.

"Oh!" Taken by surprise, Layne stopped in her tracks to avoid running right into the tired-looking man who had short, salt-and-pepper hair, though it was more pepper than salt. If he had been surprised to see her standing there, it didn't show. Mick gave her a warm smile and opened his arms, "Ah, there she is! Layne, I heard you were back. You look radiant."

"Thanks, Uncle Mickey; it's nice to see you, too." She leaned forward and gave him a big ol' hug. Even well into his fifties, Mick Flannigan was built like a tank, making it difficult to fully wrap her arms around him. By that same token, his arms engulfed her all too easily.

He wasn't truly her uncle, but he may as well have been. Mick had been working for her father since before she was born. Every birthday, every holiday, every heartbreak, and every blow-out argument with her parents, he had been there.

He returned her hug with a big squeeze and a quick peck on the cheek. Before they could catch up, another more slender figure appeared beside them.

"Hey, sis." Her brother, despite being almost a year younger than she was, looked like he had aged twice as much in the four years she had been gone. It was all in his eyes—he had seen some serious shit. The type of shit that saturates your soul with an inconceivable darkness.

Mick patted the back of Layne's shoulder as he walked off down the hall.

Liam didn't offer a hug and instead kept his hands inside the pockets of his black dress slacks. "Surprised to see you so soon. Figured you'd want to settle in and catch up with your friends first." The tone of his voice said it all; he wasn't going to be the one throwing her a homecoming celebration. That was fine by her.

Getting on the defensive, she crossed her arms in front of her chest and gave an indifferent shrug. "Family first, right?" Her tone was dry and unamused to match the tension between her and her little bro.

Before things stewed much longer, a large hand grasped Liam's shoulder. Her father appeared beside his son, "Go help Mick with the arrangements for our meeting this evening."

As usual, there were no requests from her father—only orders. Liam nodded, but then tossed Layne a smirk, "Sure, glad to do my part to keep the family business running smoothly." He had to make that final jab before he followed Mick down the hall. Layne shook her head in utter annoyance before turning her attention back to her father.

Just shy of six feet, he was an average-looking man. The beginnings of grey hairs were fading in right near his ears, contrasting with the rest of his light auburn hair. His custom grey suit didn't hold a single wrinkle and had probably cost more money than most cars.

"Layne, sweetheart, I can't tell you how much I missed you." His arms surrounded her in a loving and affectionate hug.

"Hi Dad, I missed you too. I've been looking forward to coming home and doing my part to help around here." She offered him an excited smile and he matched it with a smile of his own. He wrapped a single arm around her shoulders and guided her into his office, shutting the door behind them.

"It makes me so happy to hear you say that, Layne. I know you've wanted to be involved for a long time now. You've been incredibly patient, and for that I am grateful. After giving it a lot of thought," Scott finally parted from her and made his way around his massive wooden desk to ease into an oversized leather chair, "I have come up with the perfect fit for you."

Could she believe her ears? Was her father finally going to let her join in on the business dealings? Her thoughts were already racing to try and figure out what her role could be. Maybe it would involve managing some client relationships on her own, pulling in a commission of payments collected. Her thoughts were ricocheting all over the place inside her head at the potential.

Ultimately, it didn't matter which assignment he was going to give her, she was going to excel at it like the stubborn perfectionist she was. She may have been a petite young woman, but she knew not only how to defend herself, but how to physically get her point across to those who needed some 'convincing'. Layne wasn't above using violence where it was needed, that's for sure.

Her dad continued speaking while Layne's eyes lit up in anticipation of getting what she had always wanted, "With your degree in business administration, there's a lot I could use your help with, but not nearly as much as you can help Bryan Madigan."

Suddenly, she was very unclear about where this train was heading. Layne furrowed her brows and tilted her head slightly, "Ian's son?"

Scott nodded his head. "Yes. He's heading a large project for us and could use your skillset. After talking with Ian, it became clear that you and Bryan would work together nicely. Once you two are legally married, you can help take charge of the assets in his family's name and keep it looking good as far as Uncle Sam is concerned."

"Wait. I'm sorry, what?" It was as if someone dropped

the floor out from underneath her. Had he just said something about marriage?

"What do you mean married?" She hadn't escaped her family's affinity for having a short fuse and vicious temper and it showed, her voice escalating in volume.

"I didn't want to spring this on you as soon as you got here, but if we rush to get this done before year-end it would look spectacular during tax season. You know what I mean?"

It was the beginning of September, and he wanted her to marry some guy within the next four months? There he was, sitting in that massive chair, talking about her future as though it was just another business transaction. When she said she wanted to be involved, she hadn't meant getting married off to a guy she only knew by name. Layne had expected something a little more…illegal.

"No." It was a full sentence emphasized with a shake of her head.

"Now, Layne, I sent you to a damn good school, and you're telling me you don't understand how marriage and assets work? How this would benefit everybody's wallet?"

"No, as in I'm not marrying him. In fact, I'm not marrying anybody. I told you that when I got back here, I wanted a respectable role in this family," she emphasized the respectable part.

She continued, "Being hooked up with one of your lackey's kids was not and has never been what I meant!" She went from feeling like her heart had sunk into the basement, to feeling her rage erupting through the proverbial roof. Layne was allowing her temper to rear its fiery head.

Scott looked at her without any visible emotion, as though he had expected this level of response.

"I missed the part where I asked whether or not you had an opinion on this. You wanted a role, and I am giving you one that is an appropriate fit for you. He will be over for dinner tonight. You can get to know him on more of a personal level."

Her hand angrily lashed out and swiped at the pencil holder on the corner of his desk, knocking it clear across the room with various writing utensils scattering through the air before dropping to the beige carpet.

She screamed at him, "This is bullshit!"

Layne's dad hadn't changed one bit. She stormed out of the office, swinging the door open so hard it gave a reverberated clatter against the stopper behind it.

Layne passed Liam on her way toward the front door. He had a shit-eating grin on his face, clearly knowing what their father had lined up for her.

"I hear congratulations are in order for the future Mrs. Madigan." He even snorted in amusement seeing her clear discontent at the situation.

"Fuck you, Li!" Harshly she shoved him, hoping to knock that snarky look off his face.

The shove had more strength behind it than he had been expecting, causing him to stumble a step back. In typical O'Reilly fashion, his ugly temper reared up and he stepped up to her, shouting in her face. "You're just pissed because you're more valuable as a hot piece of ass than—" She didn't let Liam finish that sentence.

Her fist connected and followed through with the side

of his face. He dropped to the floor and before she could strike again, two barrels for arms encircled her waist and drew her back. Layne's legs kicked to squirm out of the lock hold.

"You're a piece of shit, Liam! You've been riding dad's coattails since we were kids! You've had it all handed to you because you're not man enough to do it on your own!" It may have been harsh, but from Layne's point of view, it was the solid truth.

She was getting pulled back further and further away from Liam, who was now sitting up groggily as his hand rubbed his temple. As for Layne, Mick had her off near the staircase a few feet away. Finally, he set her down on her feet and stood in front of her, blocking her path. "Alright, alright, knock it off."

Layne was fuming as she stood there, but she knew damn well she wasn't going to be able to get around Mick. That was, not without trying to throw a punch at him too.

After witnessing the entire situation unfold, Scott stood outside his office door rubbing the bridge of his nose as the impending headache descended upon him. "Mick, call Ian and cancel tonight's dinner."

Dinner wasn't the only thing that got canceled. Shortly thereafter, her father canned the engagement as well. It was painfully evident to the O'Reilly patriarch that his daughter had far too much of his spirit in her to be cast off to the side, all because he wanted to spare her from being exposed to the same life of organized crime that had robbed him of his wife.

CHAPTER TWO

Present day

The past three years had been a whirlwind of highs and lows. Finally, Layne was getting her way and making a name for herself in the O'Reilly family business. It started with small tasks such as picking up and dropping off packages, graduated to being present during discussions with folks who were late on debts owed, and then slowly she was given the blessing to be free to negotiate terms and collect debts on her own. Recently, she began playing an integral role in strategic planning and advanced discussions in evolving their enterprise to the next level.

Scott had insisted that she continue to work with some of his top men to refine her ability to physically defend herself and fine-tune her expertise with various weapons. She hit the gym regularly and worked with weights to keep her strength up to par as well as cardio to ensure she had endurance worth a damn.

These days, Layne had her hands in a little bit of everything when it came to projects she managed. She was like a bit of honey with a killer bee sting: she could assist in negotiations by supplying that charming smile of hers or be the small but mighty strike.

A lot of her interactions had been mostly with weak, small-minded, white-collared businessmen that pissed their pants the second you brandished a gun in their presence. Of course, she had her own learning curve of understanding when to reign in her hot-headedness.

Liam was still being groomed to take the lead over the entire enterprise, which was fine by Layne as she had zero interest in being the head boss lady. Over time, the tension between her and her younger sibling eased up. He had done a lot of maturing, and Layne had been willing to give him the space to earn her respect while he worked on proving himself capable of his eventual promotion. There were still those days though when she wanted to smack the crap out of him for his holier-than-thou attitude.

She had woken up to her phone buzzing on her nightstand. Wearily, she answered and immediately regretted it when she was informed that today was not going to go as she had planned. Layne expected to sit in her feelings today, drink heavily, and wallow in solitude. It was the one day of the year she allowed herself to come undone. Instead, she had to get herself up out of bed and take care of a small matter down in Chelsea.

Layne ended up paying a visit to one of her more problematic clients, George Sallakis, who was about as shady as they came. He was a small-time attorney with a big-time ego problem. Surprising for a lawyer, huh? However, he was conveniently useful when it came to handling any run-ins with the law. The number of times charges were dropped thanks to his connections was invaluable, and her family richly compensated him for it.

There was the expectation per their agreement that he was on retainer solely for the O'Reillys and keeping the details of their delicate matters to himself. Yet, intel was drifting in that he was passing highly sensitive information freely between the two biggest factions of the criminal underworld in the city: the O'Reillys and the Franzettis.

The Franzettis were headed up by one supremely arrogant Michael Franzetti. Michael, by comparison to Scott, was less old-school about how he operated his business. He got his hands dirty, occasionally using outside resources that weren't in his circle of trust, and as long as those hired resources got things done, he didn't give a shit how they accomplished it.

Sometimes these hands Michael hired were some thug-wannabe that was sloppy as fuck. Why did the O'Reillys care about the way Franzetti handled his business? It put all the city's factions at risk thanks to these punk kids having no loyalty, no respect, drawing far too much attention to themselves, and having no ability to intelligently execute a simple assignment without collateral damage.

As for poor little Georgie, he had made the mistake of getting drunk and bragging to a hooker about how he was raking in all the dough from double-crossing the two largest elite factions in the city. That particular hooker just so happened to be on the O'Reilly books for exclusive entertainment for extraordinarily important clientele. More importantly, she was Liam's own personal booty call. When Liam got the word from his favorite piece of ass, she was rewarded very generously for her contribution.

Layne found herself leaning forward, her hands on the edge of George's cheap metal desk in his musty-smelling office. Files were scattered haphazardly across the top of the desk, the computer monitor collecting a layer of dust on the back of it, and a half-drunk cup of coffee sitting on top of a pile of papers. Framed certifications and licensures hung crookedly on the wall. It was amazing this man had any level of competency, based on the state of affairs of where he spent his time working.

"George, I am having a *really* bad start to my day. Do you want to know why?"

He was held down by his shoulders in the creaky office chair on the other side of the desk by two of Layne's muscled helpers. He shook his head, a bead of sweat slowly rolling down his temple.

"Let me tell you. I was supposed to have today off for some critically important self-care. I even had a spa day scheduled that I booked for myself six months ago, but I had to cancel because I received some very troubling information. I heard that you might have been running your mouth to the wrong fuckin' people. A slutty little bird told me that you've been sharing with some friends over in Franzetti's camp."

Immediately, he tried to interject with his defense, "That's not true, I—"

"Don't interrupt me with your bullshit, Sallakis." She could feel her blood pressure rising at the thought of how this was how she was spending *today* of all days, dealing with this asshat.

"I thought to myself when I was told this little piece of information that no, you couldn't possibly be that much of a moron. So, naturally, I looked into it. Imagine my surprise when I came to realize that you've been helping Franzetti's goons with get-out-of-jail-free cards. It did not give me the warm and fuzzies, George."

She frowned at him and straightened up, walking around the desk so she was now on the same side as him. She perched her ass up on the edge of the desk, resting her hands on top of her thigh.

"You've been working for us for a very long time, and you know we reward loyalty. But this?" Layne shook her head with a sigh of straight-up disappointment. George sat there, getting antsy in his seat like he had roaches crawling up his legs.

"You don't understand," he responded in a panic, quick to plead his case to her. "They were threatening my sister and her family. I didn't have a choice."

"You're right, I don't understand. But that's the easy part of my job here, George. I don't have to understand. You could have come to us first and let us handle things. Instead, you run off and stab us in the back after all we've done for you. The Benz you have out front? Wasn't that a generous Christmas bonus last year?"

"It-it was, and I am beyond g-grateful," he stuttered.

This was the part of her job that never got any easier, but the message they had to send was crystal clear. Double-crossing Layne's family resulted in swift and severe punishment. A few years ago, she might have let it bother her, but now? Layne had become numb to ridding the world of a little evil on occasion.

"I wish I could say this will hurt me more than it will hurt you." Layne dug around in her pocket, pulled out a silver lighter, and tossed it to the bulky man to the right of the traitor. "Let it burn," she ordered as she slid off the edge of the desk.

"W-wait! No! It's a big misunderstanding! I can fix this! I can make it right!" George shouted at her while the two men began to forcibly restrain him to the office chair at the wrists and feet. As for Layne? She had given her command, and her two lackeys were following it. There was nothing left for her to do other than make her exit.

Moments later, her associates joined her outside the quaint office building while she leaned back against the side of George's freshly washed Benz and stared. Within minutes, smoke was beginning to seep out of the building, followed by flames licking at the curtains in the windows.

Such a shame, Layne thought. One less scumbag lawyer in the world.

CHAPTER THREE

This morning's unexpected meeting hadn't changed the fact that she still had been looking forward to this much-needed day to herself. It was a day where booze of any type was a requirement, not just thanks to George's demise.

Every year on this particular day was reserved for mind-numbing drinking until all the feelings folded in on themselves. All of this meant she was going to spend her evening at McGregor's Pub until the owner, Sean, ceremoniously kicked her out.

The dive joint resided in the heart of the O'Reilly territory, making it a safe getaway for all the associates and underlings that worked for them. Layne assisted the bar with keeping the books clear of any red flags, and in return, there was a no-questions-asked policy when there were business discussions taking place.

McGregor's was said to be one of the oldest bars in Manhattan, established in 1854. The exterior had a green sign above the door with its name written in a Gaelic-styled font, the façade was black with massive glass windows on either side of the two black doors of the entrance. To the right of the door flew the Irish flag, and to the left was the proud Star-Spangled Banner.

Once inside, the ragged and run-down charm was plastered from floor to ceiling. The walls had nearly no bare space due to the plethora of framed photos taken of patrons over the years. The front half of the establishment had a handful of wooden tables to the left, a narrow walkway in the center, and a well-used wooden bar to the right. Past the bar, into the back half of the pub was a second room that held a few more tables and allowed for more privacy and discretion.

Part of the innate appeal of McGregor's was that it also did not install any televisions, didn't have WiFi, was dimly lit, and was thoroughly stuck in its ways.

Sitting at the bar as far back from the doors as possible, Layne stared into the depths of the dark ruby liquid in her pint glass that most people mistook for a thick black beer. Her sparkling emerald-colored eyes were locked on the heady stout as the reflections of the lights above shifted into a daydream of memories. One memory in particular ravaged her brain.

"Layney, which snack would you like? I have chocolate chip cookies or vanilla pudding," both were homemade by her mother, Shannon, who had a knack for finding her way around the kitchen.

Her mother was to thank for the green eyes Layne inherited. Shannon had been a very attractive and classy woman. Even knowing what Scott did for a living, she brought out the best in him where she could. Everything Layne's brain could recall about her mother was the epitome of pure innocence and overwhelming love.

She could remember her mom standing there by the kitchen counter, ready to dish up whichever snack a then five-year-old Layne desired.

"I want the peanut butter cookies you always buy."

"Honey, we don't have any more. You have to wait until I go to the store to get some."

"But I want some now!" Even back then, that trade-mark temper and hard-headedness flared up. Of course, her mom knew the best way to do damage control before the waterworks started pouring out of little Layne's eyes.

Shannon drew in a calming breath and placed her hands lightly on Layne's shoulders as she lovingly looked at her daughter. "How about this? I will go to the store and pick up cookies, but you need to go upstairs to your room and have it spotless by the time I get back. Sound like a fair deal?"

Little Layne sniffled and was quick to nod her head. Her mother came in closer and wrapped her arms around Layne, drawing her into a warm embrace, and pressed a kiss to her forehead.

That moment likely only lasted a second or two, but in Layne's mind, it had lasted for an eternity.

"Sweetheart," the voice was no longer the delicate and feminine one of her mother. Instead, it was deeper and raspy. "Hey, sweetheart."

Layne snapped out of her head and was back there

sitting at the bar in McGregor's. She blinked a few times and noticed the owner and current bartender, Sean, was staring at her from behind the bar. He must have been in his seventies and was the one trying to flag her attention.

Slowly her lips curved into a weakly held smile, "Sorry, it's been a long week."

"I gotta go in the back and fix a tap line. Shout if you need something, eh?"

Layne nodded. "Got it," as she lifted her glass to her lips and took a hefty sip to help diminish the pain of the past, the pain that started fifteen years ago today.

The gruff and shaggy-haired man made his way into the back, disappearing from sight.

It was a quiet Tuesday night inside the pub. The music playing from the speakers in the ceiling was only at a volume loud enough to blend into background noise, a few businessmen were at the circular four-top in the back corner with their ties hanging loose around their necks while they talked shop amongst themselves, and the ceiling fan's pull chain lightly tapped against the bare light bulb as the fan blades slowly spun round and round. It may not have been a fancy spot, but nobody bothered her here.

The soft ring of a bell sounded off as the front door was pushed open, allowing a caressing breeze of fresh air to slip inside. A man who looked rough around the edges, who easily was in his mid-to late thirties stepped inside the establishment. Layne didn't bother taking her eyes off the pint in front of her.

She picked up on the sound of the stool next to her being dragged across the floor a few inches and felt the new presence perch on it right beside her. Didn't people have common decency anymore? The entire rest of the bar had seating available, and this person couldn't at least sit one more seat over as a courtesy as to not encroach on her personal bubble?

Not too long after the newcomer settled in, the husky scent of sage and leather drifted her way. It was pleasant on the senses, not aggressively applied, and for a brief moment, made her want to lean in a little closer.

"Who do you have to kill to get a drink 'round here?" The stranger next to her spoke up. His voice bore a tone that prickled at her most intimate desires. It wasn't clear who he was speaking to. One thing was painfully clear, he had never stepped foot inside this place before.

Here's the thing about McGregor's; it was always the same damn crowd, which had its pluses and minuses. It was rare to have new faces finding themselves coming in here. Not only was it off the beaten path and had an aesthetic that looked worse for wear, but it also had an ill-conceived reputation. Her family may or may not have had something to do with all that.

Tiredly, Layne set her pint down on the counter and drew in a breath, transforming it into a forced smile as she looked over the guy next to her, "First time?"

The moment her eyes focused on him, the air in her lungs vanished as she temporarily forgot how to breathe. Across his square jaw was a light layer of scruff, dirty blonde hair haphazardly styled longer on top and shorter on the sides, eyes the color of bitter dark chocolate, and a body that screamed either prison time or professional model.

It was just a hunch, but from the look of the tattoo creeping up the side of his neck, it was likely the former. The inked wings on the side of his neck wasn't the only tattoo either. The tops of his hands and fingers also had various images and symbols etched into his flesh. Without leaning over and appearing as intrigued as she truly was, the only piece of art she could make out was a thorny stem and the bottom half of a toothy grin of a skull before the sleeve of his jacket concealed the rest of it.

Her very core immediately reacted to the easy-on-the-eyes stranger situated next to her. A sense of excitement was building as she realized that he wasn't part of the typical clientele that came to this spot.

The man was dressed in a pair of work boots, rugged jeans, a black tank, and a silver chain draped around his neck that disappeared into his shirt. To top it all off was a black leather jacket that looked well-worn in multiple aspects. The day may have suddenly started looking up.

Layne internally appreciated the fresh face but avoided entanglements with random men she met at shady, rundown bars - even here at McGregor's. Those types of guys were the ones that were more trouble than they were worth. This one looked like a hell of a lot more trouble than average, that's for sure. The temptation to break her own rule was already beginning to taint her thoughts.

He didn't even try to hide the fact he gave her a solid once-over from head to toe. All he did was smirk. "It hasn't been my first time since I was fourteen." There was the not-so-subtle insinuation that he wasn't talking about his first visit to McGregor's anymore. Oh, yes, this one had epically bad news written all over him. Layne wondered how many hearts he had broken in the last month alone. If she had a heart to break, she would love to see him try.

"Oh, be still my heart. I bet that type of charm gets all the girls dropping their panties for you," she mockingly replied, a hand coming to her chest for a dramatic gesture.

Amused, he leaned in a little closer to her so she could inhale a little more of that intoxicating cologne, "You offering?"

Cocky son of a bitch. Attempting to keep her head on straight, Layne quickly changed the topic before it devolved any further. "If you want a drink, rest assured that you won't need to commit a felony. Sean is in the back, he'll be out in a minute."

"In that case," the stranger leaned over the bar and reached into the well, lifting up a bottle of whiskey and grabbing a rocks glass on the nearby drying plate. Layne perked an eyebrow as she stared in disbelief, wondering if this guy was for real as he began pouring the amber liquid into the glass for himself.

"You can't just..." she initially struggled to pull together a coherent thought as he thought he could just help himself to a drink here.

"What do you think you're doing?" She snatched the bottle out of his hand and set it down on the other side of her. "You don't just walk in here and serve yourself." Given her family's oversight of McGregor's books and business, she felt duty-bound to protect their asset. Layne scoffed that he had the balls to think he could do as he saw fit.

All she got back in response from him was an entertained grin, and he raised the glass of whiskey in the air slightly, "Cheers." He downed the mouthful of booze followed by extending his hand out towards her, "Joey. Joey De Luca."

With his hand outstretched towards her she blinked a few times, skeptically looking it over. So, the skull tattoo on his hand indeed continued up towards his wrist. Across its head were deep red petals of a rose sitting there like a floral crown. Finally, she extended her hand to him, but before she could give it a shake, he embraced it and drew it to his lips where a delicate kiss was laid on her knuckles.

Was he trying to be some sort of knight in shining armor pulling out all the moves in an attempt to woo her? It may have been just a little effective as her cheeks fostered a slight warmth. Men didn't go to such lengths to get her attention, nor did she go around looking for those that did. Typically, it was just a catcall or in some cases a decision to lay a smack on her ass. Both instances always ended poorly for the guy. Dating apps were so much easier for weeding out some of the assholes.

"I'm Layne." Her skin was still tingling where he had kissed her, and she was trying her damnedest not to pay any attention to it. She was utterly failing at the latter.

"It's a pleasure to meet you, Layney." The way he uttered the word 'pleasure' felt intentionally intimate, especially as his hand was still embracing hers. His thumb rubbed over her fingers idly.

Layne pulled back her hand from his before her hormones got any more bright ideas, more so than they already were. Today was not about getting laid, but damn if the universe wasn't trying to make it happen.

"Don't call me 'Layney'." That nickname was what her mother had always called her, and now it was just too painful to let anyone else have the privilege.

"Why not? I think it suits you." Joey ran his tongue over his lips as those inviting brown eyes took in the sight of her again.

"Because, then I'd have to kick your ass out of here. I wouldn't want you to suffer that embarrassment." She smirked at him, knowing that she had bruised a metric ton of male egos. Joey wouldn't be the first, and he wouldn't be the last.

He chuckled. "I'd like to see a little thing like you try. You're what? Five-foot?"

"Five-one." She rolled her eyes after correcting him. "You're what? Like six-foot with three inches below the belt?"

Apparently, his ego wasn't easily bruised. Instead of taking offense, he bantered back. "Six-two and I will let you check what's below the belt right now." His hand moved down to the waist of his pants, tugging on the tail of his belt, willing to prove her assessment of his other measurements wrong.

Layne's hand nearly knocked over her pint glass in an effort to brace herself as he seemed ready to just whip himself out right then and there. Quickly, she stabilized the drink and moved it off to the side to prevent any other potential spills.

Before she could come back with a snarky comment,

her cell phone in her pocket began going off. Taking it out of her pocket, she looked at the caller's name and cursed underneath her breath. She placed the phone up to her ear as she answered in the sweetest voice she could muster. "Hey."

But before she could get another word out, the caller on the other end immediately began to go off on her, leaving it difficult to get a word in edgewise. "No, I—Yes, but—If you'd let me—" She pressed her lips together in a hard line, attempting to restrain herself from lashing back verbally.

Finally, after a few more minutes that dragged on she was able to speak up. "I understand. I will take care of it. Bye, Liam." Layne hung up and returned the phone to where it came from.

"Ouch, somebody out past curfew?" This guy just thought he was so funny, didn't he?

"Haven't you heard of staying in your lane?" She retorted. There was no time wasted in finishing off the last of her pint. Pulling out a twenty-dollar bill, she left it next to the now barren glass. Meanwhile, she could feel Joey's eyes still locked on her. She was already agitated from that unpleasant phone call and not so politely reacted to his stares. "What are you looking at?"

He casually shrugged and shook his head. "Nothing. Just observing."

"Well, don't. There's nothing to observe." She took off towards the exit, but before she reached the door a set of strong hands wrapped around her waist and spun her around, taking her by surprise. Layne found herself staring up into Joey's eyes as he towered over her figure by over a foot.

There was a burning heat in the way he looked at her that caused an ache that she didn't expect between her legs. It was unclear how long it was that both of them stood there looking at one another, saying nothing at all. Finally, she broke the silence, and her words managed to only sound slightly breathless. "I have to go."

It wasn't her most profound statement of the night, but it was the truth.

"Before you run outta here, how about you at least give me the chance to buy your next round another night?"

She stared up at that incredibly handsome face, searching for a reason not to take him up on his offer. "Leave your number with Sean, and I will call you the next time I'm looking for a guy to make bad decisions with."

Amusement in his grin, his face lowered down closer to her, prompting Layne to squirm out of his grasp at the very last second before he had the opportunity to make any big mistakes.

Without looking back, she hurriedly left the pub, mentally reassuring herself that it was the best course of action. Guys like Joey may have been good for a one-time romp, but they often came with a shit ton of baggage. Layne had enough of her own baggage to carry around, she didn't need complications from someone else's.

Once the cool night air hit her face, Layne focused on putting one foot in front of the other. Why was she so stirred up? It was one guy. One stupid, annoying guy. She shook her head, mentally scolding herself for being so caught up in this.

Despite the temptation, Joey didn't follow after her and instead hung back at McGregor's to order another round of firewater after Sean returned from fixing the equipment. He wrote his number down as instructed, pushing the slip of paper over towards the bartender.

Any other night he would have shot his chance and followed after Layne, but he had other obligations on his agenda for the evening. He had only come in here to piss away some time because it had been conveniently located on the way to his next appointment. That appointment was a particularly important job he had to get to in an hour's time, and he didn't want to be late. He really hated being late.

CHAPTER FOUR

Layne arrived at the parking garage one block down from the pub and pulled out her keys from her jacket pocket to her vehicle which was parked there on the ground floor. It didn't take long to realize that her steps weren't the only ones tapping against the concrete. There was a light shuffle following behind her.

Giving a huff and a sigh she stopped in her tracks. "Look, I don't have time for this."

She turned around ready to give Joey a piece of her mind. That's when she felt the heavy palms slam into the front of her chest in a violent shove, causing her to stumble backward. Instead of falling straight onto her ass, a set of bulging arms locked around her, pinning her arms down to her sides.

Instantly her body triggered its fight or flight mode, and she was sure as hell ready to get into a fight. The edgy feeling was very familiar to her. Adrenaline caused her heartbeat to pound like a war drum inside of her ears while her thoughts raced frantically to assess the threat.

"Get the fuck off of me!" Her foot stomped down onto the stranger's foot followed by an elbow thrusted back into his squishy stomach. Layne found temporary freedom from Squishy Guts, only to have the first attacker grab her by the throat and toss her down onto the ground.

Her body fell onto the unforgiving surface with enough momentum that she rolled over once. As she was rolling onto her back, she was able to free her 9mm Shield from the inside of her jacket holster. These days, she didn't leave home without it.

Before she could steady the aim of the pistol it was kicked right out of her grasp. It skittered across the concrete underneath a nearby Corolla parked several yards away. Now she found herself lying there on the ground, weaponless, staring at two very pissed-off men. They both had guns drawn, pointed directly at her.

Layne kept her hands out in front of her and didn't make any sudden movements. Who knew how itchy their trigger fingers were? She sure as hell didn't want to find out.

"What the hell do you want?"

Ignoring her question, the averagely-built bald one barked at her while keeping his weapon's sight locked on her. "Get up, bitch."

When she didn't move right away, his partner who looked like he had eaten one too many creme puffs leaned down, and with his free hand, snatched her arm with a painful squeeze before jerking her up onto her feet.

What happened after that she didn't know, but she felt the impact on the back of her head right before everything went dark.

Ouch. Her head was killing her, and there was the dull ache of what was going to grow into a bruise, if it hadn't already started. Layne attempted to assess how much of a bruise she was going to have with her fingers, but immediately came to the realization her hands were bound at the wrists in front of her by some standard zip ties. Fucking fabulous.

She gave a quiet groan in response to the pain while her eyes slowly opened. Swallowing hard, Layne tried to focus her vision. Things were moving, and it wasn't immediately clear if it was a byproduct of getting struck on the back of her head or if the movement was legitimately occurring. As her eyes began to adjust and process the surroundings, it was evident that much time couldn't have passed since she had been jumped in the parking garage.

Things were still cloaked in darkness, but now she was noticing the coming and going of street lamps to her right. Warm glows that approached and then passed by at semi-regular intervals. She was in a car. The scent of cigarettes, cheap air fresheners, and old takeout containers filled the air around her. It was nauseating to breathe in, or maybe that was due to a potential concussion.

When she began to shift in her seat, something jabbed into her side. Looking down, it was a gun being held by one of the men who had attacked her. Baldy to be precise. The other man, Squishmallow, was at the steering wheel transporting them all to their next destination, wherever that was.

She thought about the speed they were going and how likely it was she could jump out of a moving vehicle without getting killed.

"Don't even think about it you stupid cunt." Just to be a brat she thought about it again anyhow, not that they had to know that. After assessing the precarious situation, there were too many unknowns for her to attempt to flee. So, Layne sat still and didn't say a word. It was a rare occasion indeed.

After what may have been the longest five minutes of her life, the sedan slowed and pulled in behind a small grey building by some docks. Once it came to a complete halt, her backseat chaperone tugged her out of the car with him. Her feet stumbled on the gravel while trying to keep up in whichever direction he was heading.

All three of them approached the dimly lit building that looked like it was some sort of administrative office that was no longer actively used. The one with the big belly opened the door. "Ladies first."

Once inside, it was confirmed this place wasn't currently being used and required some dire repairs. The walls had water stains, the carpet was fraying and torn in multiple places, what little furnishings were in there looked like they were from forty years ago, and the musty smell was overpowering to the senses.

The driver of the car followed inside just a few steps behind them, shutting the door and looking out through the window to make sure they had all the privacy they required. Mr. Clean gave her a shove towards a metal folding chair facing away from the door they had just come in from. "Sit."

"Where's your 'please'?" Layne remained standing.

That was the wrong question. The back of his hand went flying across her face. Layne stumbled and lifted her hands to feel her cheek, which was now on fire. Her eyes began to water involuntarily, and she did her best to blink the tears back. She didn't want to look weak and rattled. When in fact, it was quite the opposite, the pain was only adding fuel to her fire that was flickering in her murderous glare.

Defiantly, she remained standing there refusing to take a seat just because he told her to.

"Sit, or else I will give you something better to do with that smartass mouth," he sneered lecherously at her.

Layne begrudgingly sat while she thought about which battles she wanted to pick right now with the position she was in. The driver was still standing by the door peering out the window. "Where is he? Shouldn't he be here by now?"

The bald one didn't take his gaze off her when he answered his partner. "I say we give it two more minutes before we take the lead on the job, Victor." So, the fat one had a name, wonderful. Layne now had at least one piece of useless information that she didn't have before. She wasn't sure what he meant by finishing the job but was certain she did not want to find out.

The silence in the room wasn't just uncomfortable but

felt like it was growing louder with each second that passed.

Even though she didn't have any visibility of the window behind her, she knew a car had just pulled up in front of the building. There was the crunch and roll of gravel sounding off underneath the tires, and then it came to a stop.

An authoritative pound came against the door. Victor looked at Mr. Magoo with a curt nod, confirming their expected guest had arrived before opening the door for the newcomer.

The door swung open, and a seemingly lofty figure stepped inside. With her back to the entrance, all she could rely on was the dancing of shadows against the floor and walls. The sound of heavy-duty boots thudded against the floor; Layne was willing to bet it was the man of the hour.

Conflicted on whether she should have felt a sense of relief that this third individual had arrived to join the party or not, Layne found minimal comfort that at least she didn't have to worry about whatever sick thoughts Baldy was having. Or maybe she was just being delusional.

After she assessed what was around her, and knowing her hands were mostly unavailable, the options were very limited. The upside was she still had her feet. The downside was right now it was three against one.

She heard a few husky whispers going back and forth behind her. Then, the heavy footsteps drew nearer. The sound stopped directly behind her, creating an over-whelming sensation of dread spilling over her.

A new voice broke the silence. "Is this the girl the boss was talking about?"

"Yeah. A real pain in the ass, too."

Layne couldn't help but scoff at her attacker's personality assessment of her.

"You think something's funny?" The hairless man began to step forward to make another move at her. Before he could jump on the opportunity, the newcomer reached out and stopped him with a hand bracing against his chest.

"Go get some fresh air with Victor." There was a long pause before the man at her side reluctantly left. Then, there was a light click of the door latching shut moments later.

Layne sat in the cold and rigid folding chair willing herself not to show any signs of frayed nerves. She had been in some shit before, but never on her own and never at this level of seriousness. She took another hard swallow when she felt the man's hands settle on top of her shoulders from behind and squeeze them firmly. Now it was just the two of them there.

She jerked her shoulders to attempt shrugging off his grip. It was a failed attempt as he pulled her to sit back in the chair. He didn't have to say any words, instead, it was clear that he was trying to ensure she was intimidated. Knowing all about the effective use of intimidation tactics, she knew that he was doing a decent job of using them.

There was something familiar lingering in the air, but she couldn't quite pinpoint it. Not to mention, now didn't seem like the time to assess the minor details when bigger problems were going on here, like survival. Survival would be good.

The large pair of hands eventually released her shoulders, and the man circled 'round from the back of her seat to stand in front of her. He was decked out in all-black tactical clothing from his boots, up to the cargo pants that hugged his muscular thighs, a long-sleeved shirt with black gloves on his hands, up to the mask covering the lower half of his face from right under his eyes downward past his chin, and a knit cap over the top of his head. The only exception to the all-black ensemble was that the mask had white markings on it to mimic the bottom half of a skull's nose, jaw, and teeth.

When this new threat came to stand in front of her, his body went rigid for a split moment. It was indiscernible as to why.

Layne stubbornly refused to show any fear and coldly locked her gaze right on him. He leaned over with one gloved hand roughly grabbing her jaw as he gave a hard stare right back at her. "It's just you and me now, princess. I'm only going to ask my questions one time, and you're going to be a good girl and answer them."

His voice rang low on the register with a dark undercurrent that suggested he was going to make good on any threats he made.

"Good luck with that." Layne wasn't going to give this theatric creep the time of day.

He chuckled in amusement at her confidence. "Now, tell me your name." The strength of his hand prevented her from turning her face away from him, though she tried. His fingers digging into her cheeks were starting to become uncomfortable, even with her tolerance for discomfort.

"Betty White."

He growled under his breath, releasing her jaw only to pull her up onto her feet by her upper arm. The masked man spun her around, wrapping one thick muscled arm around her waist, pinning her arms against her, and forcing her back against his chest. That's when she felt the cold of a steel blade up against the bare skin of her throat. This man was a different breed than the other two individuals standing guard outside.

Her chest rose and fell heavily with her labored breaths as her fear spiked. Layne's body tensed and she strained to keep her neck away from the sharp edge of the knife. She didn't manage to get very farm except leaning further back against the brick wall of his torso.

The coarse fabric of the mask brushed up against her ear and through the mask's material, she could feel the warmth of his breath and smell the light scent of really cheap whiskey. "Do you want to reconsider your answer? I would be a good little girl if I were you."

He dropped his voice down to a whisper, "You don't want to find out what I do to bad girls."

"And you don't want to find out what I do to deranged psychopaths." Her retorts were one of the few things that kept her from giving in to straight-up panic.

He tsked at her response, the knife now starting to apply more pressure against her throat, prompting her to wince and draw in a sharp breath. The acknowledgment of defeat began to creep in, and she took a second to steady her voice. Still, it didn't come out as strong as she would have liked. "It's Layne."

The masked man lightly dragged the tip of the blade along the length of her neck, the weapon threatening to break her skin if she so much as thought of speaking too loudly. "Mm, thank you. What's your last name, Layne?"

The way he spoke her name made her feel something deep inside of her that should have been illegal. She hesitated to respond to him, knowing damn well her family name could be a toss-up in either getting her out of trouble or catapulting her into a shit ton of it.

He wasn't feeling very patient with her. The blade was removed for a split second, only for him to turn her to face him. His left hand grabbed a handful of the back of her silky strands of chestnut hair, tugging harshly so her throat was more exposed to him. The knife returned to its spot against the delicate skin covering her carotid artery.

"I can see your pulse in your neck. Do you know how excited that makes me?" If Layne hadn't figured it out before now, it was confirmed that this man was definitely on another level of unhinged, unpredictable, and dangerous. Perhaps even as much as she was.

"O'Reilly. My last name is O'Reilly." She didn't need an unstable individual getting too antsy to spill her blood before she could strategize an escape.

"That's a good girl. Let's continue behaving, Layney, and this will be more enjoyable for us both." He didn't release her or lower the knife. Instead, he remained in his current position, and unless he was packing a lot more distinct weapons, it was clear he was getting plenty of enjoyment out of this from what she could feel.

The interrogation continued. "What is the 227 project?" He dragged the knife down over her collarbone in a slow and intentional movement.

Genuinely confused, she wrinkled her brows, "The 227 project? I have no fucking clue. Sounds like a terrible band name." The masked assailant was silent for what felt like an eternity, so Layne decided now would be the time to try and stall to buy herself more time for a miracle opportunity to make a move.

"I swear, I have no idea what it is. Please, don't hurt me." She dialed up the emotions that danced over the words she spoke to appeal to any sliver of humanity he had. "I can get you money - however much you need."

Her father's words of wisdom to her, etched into her brain from a young age, were on repeat in her head; exhaust every option to escape from a bad situation, it is better to risk potential death than to do nothing and make it definite.

"Shut up." His words weren't yelled but they held a commanding tone to them. He needed to reassess if it was possibly true that she had zero knowledge of the project. His intuition told him that she wasn't lying, not about this anyway.

The blade was taken away from her throat and rehomed back into a sheath at his hip. During that brief window of an opportunity where he didn't have the knife readily available, Layne willed herself to make her move. She thrusted her foot in a front kick directly at his belt buckle, driving the force from her hips. The angle wasn't ideal, but it was better than nothing.

Taken off guard by the impact of her kick, his footing yielded, and he grunted upon contact. His hand released her as he bent over, drawing in a sharp breath while his hand held the temporary discomfort of his stomach.

She turned and burst into a sprint for the only way out of this hellhole. Running with your hands bound together in front of you isn't as efficient as one would like, but she had to go with what things were. No, she didn't have a plan for what she'd have to deal with on the other side of the door, but she had to handle one problem at a time.

Her fingertips had just grazed the stainless steel door handle before her body was lifted by the waist, feet coming off the ground. Her legs kicked wildly as she yelled like a banshee. "Let me go!"

The struggling and thrashing seemed to have little impact as the skull-masked man utilized his strength to carry her back to where she had been previously seated. He harshly exhaled as he dropped her onto the ground in front of the folding chair.

"Stay!" He yelled at her. "Goddamn, woman!" He groaned, making it clear he was still feeling quite uncomfortable from the unexpected shot she made and pissed off about it.

Layne tried to steady her breath as she now found herself on her ass on the cold and damp floor looking up at him. "What are you going to do to me? I don't know shit about your stupid project."

She expected an answer involving torture and death, but

he said nothing as he looked down at her. Something switched in his demeanor, and what came out of his mouth next was not what she expected.

"…Fuck." A sigh followed.

"I'm…sorry?" Layne was confused as to what part of her question had given him this pause. As much as she wanted to take credit for whatever crisis he was having, she wasn't sure that she could.

He yanked his mask down away from his face to around his neck and knelt on one knee in front of her. Revealing his face was never something he did while working his assignments, it was part of the many protective measures he took to keep an added layer of safety for himself. Even those who hired him went through an intermediary and didn't get to see him without the getup.

One look at that face underneath the mask and she found herself with her jaw hanging open and in a wordless stupor.

CHAPTER FIVE

"**J**oey? You've got to be fucking kidding me." The stupid, annoyingly hot as fuck guy from McGregor's Pub. Joey. Joey motherfucking De Luca. She should have known. The scent of cheap whiskey, the boots, the eyes, and the way he called her Layney. She should have picked up on it all, but then again, she wouldn't have ever pegged him for being involved in this level of shit.

Layne felt played like a naive little fiddle. It wasn't a feeling she was accustomed to, but hell if she was going to let it happen again.

After her brain processed the sheer confusion of how they both ended up here, her speechlessness no longer became a problem. "Oh, you asshole, motherfucker, son of a bitch jackass!" There weren't enough curse words in the Merriam-Webster for her to spew at him. She swung her bound hands in his direction, but he easily captured them in his grasp and held them still.

"Stop being a little heathen! Just let me explain."

Her heart was palpitating even harder than it had been moments ago, but now it was because she was fuming. Who the hell did he think he was? Was his conversation with her in the bar all part of some scheme? There were a million questions and scenarios zipping through her mind.

Each attempt to physically lash out at him was a failure as he expertly kept her hands still.

"Layne, give me a minute, will ya?" His eyes darted over towards the door, confirming they were still alone before looking back at her. "I didn't know it was going to be you here. Franzetti hired me, told me to come here to take care of some business, and get some answers out of you." He decidedly left out the part where he had been instructed to dump her body off the docks afterward. "Jesus, why didn't you say something at the bar earlier, huh?"

She was not going to take any fault for this. "Are you kidding me right now? What was I supposed to say? 'Oh, hey, in case you might be involved in a kidnapping later, you should know who my dad is'?"

He grumbled and rubbed his forehead while he tried to process this unforeseen complication.

"Look at me." He reached out to gently take her chin in his grasp so he could convey his intentions. "We can fix this." Joey stood up on his feet. When he tried to assist Layne up onto her own as well, she pulled back from him and did it on her own.

"We? I missed the part where this was a team effort." Her hands still clinched together via the uncomfortably hard plastic, managed to brush off the front of her pants of dirt they picked up from the likely unsanitary floor.

"Stay here." He pulled his mask back up over his face and walked away. The door creaked as it opened and shut. Not more than two minutes later, the sound repeated as he came back to her with his knife in his hand. Joey grabbed her wrists and yanked her closer to him. The tension in her body made her stiff as a board.

"Relax, I'm not going to hurt you as long as you keep your hands to yourself." Yeah, famous last words before a lot of serial killers did indeed hurt people, Layne thought.

"Don't move." She wasn't sure if it was his tone or the look in his eyes, but she fought every urge to distance herself from him as much as possible. With wary eyes, she watched as he expertly maneuvered the blade with one precise motion, slicing through the zip tie that bound her wrists together. The piece of plastic fell to the ground, and he let go of her.

She rubbed each one of her wrists now that they were experiencing freedom. Perhaps he actually was trying to help her. "Thanks." Her voice was calmer now but that didn't mean she wasn't still irritated. There may also still have been some skepticism, but she was willing to at least wait to see what was going to happen next in this grand plan of his.

"I sent Marco and Victor to the hardware store to grab a few things to buy us a little time. Here's what's going to happen; you're going to get in the Challenger out front and get the fuck out of here." Joey dug around inside his pocket and pulled out a set of keys.

She looked at the set of keys in front of her and took them. "Fine, but there's one problem."

"What's the problem?"

POP!

Layne's fist swung and made contact with Joey's jaw. It was clear it caught him off guard and left him stunned slightly. Deep down there was a bit of satisfaction of getting that out of her system after what he had put her through.

His hand rubbed his jaw. "Christ! What the hell? I'm trying to help you!"

"I figured if the story is that I got away, it should look half believable. That is, unless you're really shitty at what you do even on a good day."

Joey took Layne by the arm and escorted her to the door. "Get out of here before I realize how stupid of an idea this is."

She started to make a move to open the door, and then paused and turned to look back at him. "Why are you let—"

"Just go!" He barked at her and gave her a firm shove in the direction of the exit.

Moments later, she was in the black Challenger with tinted windows all around, the engine turning over with a roar, and the tires kicking up gravel as she got the hell out of dodge. All that was left was Joey standing there inside the building wondering how much he just fucked up.

When she was gone, he slammed his fist into the door in front of him multiple times as he yelled out in a fury of emotions. His hands then grabbed the metal chair she had been sitting in and threw it across the room. It gave a loud clatter as it crashed into the dusty desk in the corner. "Son of a bitch!"

His chest heaved up and down as the internal conflicts raged through his system. When he took jobs, he always completed them. There were never any complications, and Layne was one hell of a complication that resulted in him thinking with his dick instead of his head.

When Marco and Victor returned a little while later, he told them the fabrication of what had transpired in their absence. Joey reassured them that he would smooth things over with the big boss.

She sat in the driver's seat of the Challenger, focused on the road in front of her and constantly checked all her mirrors in a stroke of paranoia that somebody was following her. Layne's knuckles were turning white from gripping the leather-wrapped steering wheel so tightly. When she finally arrived in a safer part of town, she parked the vehicle around the corner from her townhome.

Her house was such a sight for sore eyes after the culmination of events that had transpired that evening. This had not been on her top ten list of how she pictured spending the anniversary of her mother's death.

Layne swiftly made it inside using the electronic pin pad to unlock the entrance, then immediately shut and locked the door behind her. Everything was quiet, except her mind. An overwhelming onslaught of thoughts and questions had been plaguing her mind the second she left the docks. Most importantly, why had he decided to let her go?

If what Joey had told her was true, those were Michael Franzetti's men who attacked her in the parking garage. Franzetti and her father had never been able to see eye-to-eye. Everything her father did, Franzetti either wanted to destroy it or one-up it.

It had only been in the past two years that things had settled down enough that they were able to come to some sort of arrangement to coexist. Franzetti had his defined territories in the city, and her father had his. Those boundaries were always respected by everyone on each side. McGregor's Pub and the parking garage should have been off-limits to them. Based on tonight's turn of events, the respect for the O'Reilly territory had gone dry.

Layne was tapped out - physically and mentally. Her head was banged up, a small bruise was beginning to bloom on her cheekbone where Marco had struck her, and the adrenaline rush had left her feeling entirely depleted.

Leaving the foyer, she began the slow ascent up to the second floor. After a quick shower to rinse off all the sweat and ick from her, she crawled into bed in nothing but a red camisole and panties.

There was just something about her bed that was sedative, feeling the pillow cradle her head and the blanket envelop her, it wasn't long before her eyes fluttered closed.

CHAPTER SIX

*S*he rolled over onto her back, her room cast into pitch darkness. There was a heavy weight on her bed and a presence above her. Layne's eyes opened groggily, and she saw a male figure looming over her on all fours, hands on either side of her head and his knees between her bare thighs spreading them apart. The familiar and intoxicating scent of musky leather mixed with woodsy sage overwhelmed her senses.

A dark skull mask was concealing the man's identity, but she had no doubts about whose identity it was attempting to conceal. Her hand reached up to touch his face and tug at the disguise, but his hand firmly took her wrist and pinned it above her head. His hips lowered between her legs and pressed against her center.

Layne's lips parted slightly, and a breathy moan slipped out as she felt his erection straining against his pants and pushing against her. His other hand ran up the front of her camisole, slowly grazing over her breast and right up to *her throat where she hoped maybe it was going to stop. Instead, his hand continued to travel off to the side and under her head where he grabbed a handful of her thick tresses. The masked man tugged dominantly to force her head to tilt back and in turn caused the rest of her to arch up towards his body.*

"Are you going to be a good girl and give me what I want?"

A swirling of desire and temptation rampaged deep down inside of her as he spoke with that dominating voice of his. Her body trembling with need under his touch. "Always."

"Don't lie to me, Layney." His hips began to grind up against her with purpose and sinful intentions. The thin fabric of her panties was already damp with excitement.

She whimpered and moaned out in approval with each distinct movement he made. Her pleasure was swelling, her heart was racing, and her alarm clock was buzzing.

Everything faded from the deep recesses of her subconscious and soon she was staring up at her ceiling illuminated by the sunshine pouring in from the window off to her left.

Layne groaned in despair as she smacked the alarm clock until it shut up. She didn't give a shit that it was almost ten in the morning. With conflicted feelings between her body and head, her hands covered up her face and tried to come to terms with all the feelings her dream had stirred up.

After a long, steamy shower with some desperately needed self-love, compliments of her favorite rose-shaped toy to relieve the nagging desire between her legs, Layne got dressed and went downstairs to make herself a cup of coffee.

She opted for comfort today with just a pair of black leggings and an oversized long-sleeved shirt that sloped off her shoulder. Pouring the lifesaving freshly brewed caffeine into a mug with a splash of half-and-half, she attempted to clear her mind of everything and anything related to the night before.

She stood at the kitchen sink and slowly drank the piping hot goodness while gazing out the window in front of her to focus on what her next steps were today. Keeping herself busy was going to be key to easing back into routine.

"Did you really have to park the car on the street?" A voice unexpectedly broke the silence and caused her to nearly jump out of her skin.

The mug fell from her hand, crashing into the stainless steel sink and shattering into pieces. Layne spun around to see Joey standing there at the entranceway of her kitchen, leaning against the frame with both hands in his pockets. He was dressed in a pair of well-worn jeans and a grey t-shirt that emphasized just how much effort he put into working out.

The short sleeves allowed a series of tattoos crawling up

his arms to be on full display. On the side with the skull on the back of his hand, the collage of roses, vines, and more skulls intertwined before the edge of his sleeve covered up the imagery. On the other arm, he had what appeared to be a sleeve of ravens, various clock faces, and tombstones.

"Shit!" An exasperated sigh was released as she glared over at Joey. "How did you even get in here?"

He chuckled, pushed off from the frame, and stepped further into the kitchen. "Practice."

"Wait, how long have you been here?" Suspicion rose in her voice. Layne had never been one for holding back her sounds of pleasure, especially when she thought she was home alone.

"Not long. Only came to have a chat about last night. We have some loose ends to tie up." However, there was an amusement in his eyes that indicated he might have been lying about how long he had been snooping around.

Layne raised a hand to get him to cease his talking right there. "No. There's nothing to chat about." Nothing at all. Nope. Not a thing. "You found your car, so there's no need for you to be here. Not to mention that if anyone sees you here, we'd both have hell to pay."

Joey rolled his eyes at the bossy attitude. "Look, it's not all about you, sweetheart. I risked my ass last night letting you go. So, maybe it wouldn't kill you to be a little nice and say 'thank you'."

"Thank you? That's what you came here for?" Layne scoffed in disbelief of where in the hell he got off on thinking she was going to be bowing down to him in gratitude after he just admitted to breaking and entering her house. Sure, she was grateful that things didn't get messier last night, but she wasn't about to forget that he had taken the job in the first place either.

"You're delusional. Get out." She pointed to the door.

"Not until I get what I came here for." He now stood directly in front of her. She took a step backward, feeling the edge of the center island press against her lower back. What had he come here for? Her heart skipped a beat as her mind hopped between two strikingly different scenarios; one, he came here to finish the job; or two, he was here to finish the job he had started in her dreams.

Her eyes tracked him while she held still, watching as he lessened the space between them. His hand reached past her and grabbed the keys from the countertop, then raised them in front of her face. "My mail key is on here." He gave a slight jingle of the keys in the air before dropping them into his pocket, remaining all up in her personal space - a trend that she was fairly certain she shouldn't be welcoming.

"Great, you've got your keys. Are we done here? I don't need rumors flying all over the city that I've got one of Franzetti's goons hanging around."

That made Joey outright laugh and shake his head. "One of Franzetti's goons? I'm hurt." A hand went to his chest feigning some level of offense to her assumption of who he was and what he did. "Clearly, you don't know my reputation."

Layne let out a scoff with enough attitude for ten divas. "Is that supposed to be some flex? You're some big ol' baddie and I got off easy?" He inched in closer to her, his hips just barely pressed up against her own. Holding her ground she didn't lean backwards in this little standoff they had going on in her kitchen.

"Let's get one thing straight, you got lucky. Don't expect to have it happen again. I'm the guy they call in when the bad guys are too chickenshit to get the real dirty jobs done. I don't make mistakes, I don't get involved, and I don't leave loose ends." His tone was painfully serious.

Those deep brown eyes pierced into her like daggers. Was it just Layne, or was it a little warm in here? Nobody had to tell her how bad things could have been last night. Joey had been hired to take care of the dirty work for her dad's biggest rival in this city. No matter how self-sufficient she was with handling herself, she would always be someone of value to her father and ultimately a target for enemies like Franzetti to take aim at.

"I can handle myself; don't you worry your pretty little face." Her eyes narrowed at him, and she placed her hands on the edge of the counter behind her so that she could make sure she kept them to herself.

"Is that right? Didn't look that way last night." His voice lowered as an entertained grin curved across that perfectly shaped mouth. Something dark and tempting slid into his gaze.

Layne was not going to be intimidated by anybody, especially not him. She adamantly stood her ground and maintained eye contact with him, which was starting to feel overly intimate. "I got away, didn't I?"

"You want to hear about my reputation? The ugly shit

I've done? It's not pretty. You want to know how easily you got off?"

"But, did I? Get off…easily?" A teasing sparkle shone in her eyes as the air between them began to grow heavier.

His hands grasped her sides, hoisting her up as though she weighed nothing at all, and set her ass down on the edge of the granite counter behind her. Stepping forward, he forced himself to stand between her legs, his hips making contact at the apex of her thighs.

Layne's heart was racing a mile a minute like a racehorse. Joey's face was now nearly nose-to-nose with hers. Inside her core, something else was stirring at having the warmth of his body radiating against her.

Despite the clothing separating them, she could feel how hard he was. It was delightfully head swirling. Her hands rested on top of his chest, fingers curling into the fabric of his shirt.

"Don't tempt me, Layne," he demanded. "You're not a good girl, and I'm not a good guy. I'm not the nice guy next door. I'm not your knight in shining armor. I'm not a country club twit that your dad wants you to marry." His voice came down to a whisper, his lips brushing against her own while he spoke.

Barely being able to gather her own intelligent words in response, she was proud of herself when she was able to say something semi-coherent. "Then, what type of guy are you? Hm?"

Joey may not have been the type that played golf every weekend at the local country club, but Layne saw something in him far more worthy than anything pompous asshats at the golf course could offer.

His hands ran down over the sides of her stomach and curved down over her ass, each hand taking a handful of it possessively.

As he squeezed her sweet cheeks roughly, he positioned his mouth over to the side of her throat, laying a trail of light kisses up it until he reached her ear. The heat of his breath was promising sweet, delicious, and wicked things before he finally spoke into her ear. "I'm the guy that gives you the best fuck of your life then you never see me again."

Her breath hitched and arousal was pooling between her legs. Layne's hands were grasping onto his shirt for dear life now as she prompted him. "Prove it." That was all the green light Joey needed as he gave a rumbling growl of anticipation at what he was going to do to her.

Knock, knock.

Damnit. Whatever sexual anticipation was in the air between them quickly dissipated.

Pound, pound, pound.

It wasn't Layne's heart; it was someone at her front door.

"Shit," she shoved Joey away from her, hopping off the counter and down onto her feet. Luckily, he had already read the situation and recognized he couldn't be seen there. Joey didn't hesitate to give Layne the space she needed. If anyone recognized him, it would be a major shitstorm. Being seen co-horting with his target that he had reported back as having escaped under some extraordinary circumstances would be a massive blow to his business and reputation.

"Stay here, I will go take care of it." Now she was the one giving orders, and assuming he'd have the sense to listen.

Layne went to her front door where the pounding was increasing in frequency and strength. As she drew in a deep breath to gather her composure, her hand twisted the doorknob and pulled the door open. On the front stoop was her brother, Liam. His cropped auburn hair which mirrored the same shade as their dad's, was uncharacteristically a tussled mess.

Before she got the opportunity to say anything, he pushed his way inside.

"Where the hell have you been? Are you okay?" The unpredictable level of crazy in his eyes was off the charts, even for him. He looked like he just needed to be told who had to die and he was going to send an army.

Liam stepped up to her and threw his arms around her in a suffocating hug. "Nobody has been able to get a hold of you, and given yesterday I didn't know if…" His voice trailed off, refusing to even speak the assumption out into the universe.

"I'm okay, relax." She let him practically cut off her oxygen during that hug, her hand lightly patting his back in reassurance. "I ran into some trouble and my phone got lost in the process. It was a bitch of a day, so I just wanted to pour myself a drink and pass out in bed before processing everything."

Liam's relief was quickly replaced by anger. He pulled

back and now began inspecting her for any injuries, noticing the bruise on her cheek which prompted his eyes to narrow. "What in the blessed fuck happened? Who did this?"

He didn't even wait for her account of events as he pulled out his phone to begin rallying the troops. Layne gently placed her hand on his to stop him and shook her head. "Stop Li. I never saw them before, they were looking for information on something we're not even involved in, but the important thing is that I got away and I'm fine. You know that I can handle myself." She could have given him the information that it was Franzetti's men, but she wasn't trying to rock that particular boat just yet.

Liam didn't look convinced. However, after pause and consideration, he conceded for right now. Out came an exasperated huff before he slid his phone back into his pants. "I'm going to have one of the guys keep a closer eye on you for a little bit. Just precautionary and all that. I'm sure dad would agree."

Her eyes widened slightly. "You're overreacting."

"Deal with it." Right now, he had the clout and standing in the organization to make this decision. While Layne had made progress in securing her standing, she still had to battle a lot of misogynistic attitudes.

A babysitter was the last thing she wanted, but unless she could convince Uncle Mick to side with her, it would always be Liam and her father taking the same side when it came down to it.

Now wasn't the time she wanted to bother putting up the fight, especially since she just wanted Liam on his way so she could go back and pick back up where she left off with Joey.

Finally, she convinced Liam to leave after reassuring him no less than one thousand times that she would keep every nook and cranny locked up in the house. To avoid situations like a man supercharging her sensual needs after breaking and entering into her home.

After he left, she walked into the back of the house towards the kitchen to give Joey the all-clear.

"Joey? It was just my brother, he's gone now." Then, as she found herself in a now empty kitchen, she saw the note left on the counter.

I'M NOT THE KNIGHT IN SHINING ARMOR. YOU GOT OFF EASY. -J

Layne wasn't sure why, but she felt a pang of disappointment as it was clear he had left through the back door. Glancing one more time at the handwritten note, she released a soft sigh and dropped it into the trash can. Now, all she was left with was a frown on her face at the lost opportunity and a lost chance at an orgasm or three.

Go figure that he was now the one to take off on her. Maybe it was just better off that way and it wasn't meant to be. After all, everything about him was bad news, as she had accurately predicted in McGregor's. They would be a hot mess of a match together.

The O'Reilly family highly valued loyalty and allegiances, and with Joey taking jobs from the highest bidder, his ties were only to himself. Not to mention, as he said himself, he wasn't the polo-wearing country club type her dad was set on her aligning herself with. The best-case scenario is he would never be accepted or tolerated, and the worst-case scenario? He would have a bounty hanging over his head that she couldn't protect him from.

It begged the question, why couldn't she stop thinking about him? His cocky entrance into McGregor's, the way he had ensnared her in the empty building at the docks, and the way his eyes tracked her every move.

Layne shook her head to erase the addictive thoughts of him right out of her mind.

CHAPTER SEVEN

Later in the evening, she found herself sitting at the oversized dining room table inside her father's house about a ten-minute drive north of where she resided on the Upper East Side. The formal dining room was large enough to handle fourteen guests, maybe sixteen if you squeezed some extra chairs in there. Tonight, there were only three of them occupying seats.

Her father was in the very same seat at the head of the table he was always in for as long as she could remember. Layne was sitting to his left, and across from her was Liam to the right of their dad.

Scott had invited both his children over for dinner after hearing Liam's overly dramatic briefing of what he had witnessed and heard from Layne.

He thanked the plump, black-haired maid who took away his empty dinner plate, and then sat back in his chair and looked over at Layne while swirling what was left of his Old Fashioned in the glass he held.

"You want to tell me anything?" His hand motioned to her cheek where the makeup only managed to lighten the bruise on her face.

Layne fiddled with the fork in her hand, twirling it this way and that, and then pushing around some leftover potatoes on her plate. "I already know that I don't have to. I'm sure Liam already filled you in." He always was good at tattling on her.

Liam was already about to defend his stance on all of this, but silently Scott lifted a hand to stop his son before he even started down that road. "I want to hear it from you. All of it."

She dropped her fork down onto her plate, causing a clatter that echoed in the air of the expansive room that seemed far too large for just three people to be eating in. Layne looked over at her father, letting the unspoken words build the tension.

Her father didn't move an inch while he waited for her to go ahead and respond to his initial question. She wasn't even sure he blinked.

After it was clear he wasn't going to let the subject change, she acquiesced. "Fine." Layne went ahead and gave the bare bones of her version of events, leaving everything out that had to do with Joey, and didn't drop any names of anyone else involved.

"Interesting." Her father nodded before continuing. "Nothing else to add?"

"No, I told you all that I know." She sat back in her seat, trying to find a comfortable spot in the hard wooden chair.

Mulling over everything his daughter said, Scott kept his gaze directed at her. "You mean to tell me, you don't know anything about anyone who was involved, they got the jump on you, and then you just... got away? Can you understand why I'm skeptical, Layne? You are better than this. I've taught you better than this. So, either you're lying or you're getting reckless."

She winced slightly at the tone of disappointment weighing on his words.

"Which is it, Layne? Because I can't imagine that you'd be stupid enough to lie."

Sitting there in silence, she wasn't sure what to tell him that would still keep the truth protected. Scott shook his head in disbelief that he was even having this conversation with her.

"I'm assigning a guard to keep an eye on you."

It didn't come as a surprise to her. "For how long?"

He snapped back at her with a roar. "For as long as it fucking takes for you to get some sense!" He smacked a fist onto the table, prompting a rattle out of the place settings.

Layne flinched as he lashed out. She looked at Liam across from her, he looked all smug that Dad once again took his side. Oh, how she wanted to wipe that look off his face with a handful of rusty nails, but all she could do was stare daggers at her brother before giving a pleading look to their father.

"Dad, please..."

"No, don't 'please' me. You're getting a security detail, and you're not getting any more jobs until I know you aren't going to compromise yourself or this entire damn family." Her eyes widened slightly as he tacked on that last bit that she wasn't going to be able to do any work for the organization at all.

She popped up from her seat. "What? What the hell am I supposed to do, then?"

Scott gave a tired sigh. "Layne, go out, have fun, go meet people."

"You mean go meet my future husband? Go make the rounds at all the luxury clubs, bat my eyelashes, and pretend that I want a life being cared for and providing offspring in exchange?" It sounded more like a prison sentence than any type of life she ever wanted to live.

When he didn't say anything in response to her question, she took it as confirmation that it had crossed his mind.

"Unbelievable." She gathered her belongings.

"It was a life your mother enjoyed and embraced, Layne." His attempt to make it sound more of an appealing option failed.

"No! You don't get to say that!" She pointed her finger at him. "She tolerated it! She tolerated all of this, and how was she repaid for it?" Years worth of tears filled with anger pricked at her eyes. "She got burned anyway, so don't sit there and tell me that I need to go be some damn trophy wife because it's for the better good!"

Liam tried to do his best to de-escalate the situation seeing the pain in their father's eyes at his sister's outburst. "Layne, that's not a fair comparison."

She choked back a few tears with a laugh. "The hell it isn't, Liam." Layne yanked her arms into the sleeves of her jacket and walked away from the dinner table. Both of the O'Reilly men had the sense not to agitate her further by following.

Going into the main hall, already waiting there for her was her newly assigned guard. He was going to be the first of many in the rotation of shift to shift. This one, in particular, looked like he took life way too seriously, and not the type that made having fun easy. She did her best to tell herself that all of this would blow over in a few days after everybody cooled down.

The cranky-looking guard escorted her to his car where he drove her back home, making sure to walk her inside once they got there. Mr. Uptight made himself comfortable in the living room, planning on staying in the house with her. It should have made her feel safe, but all it did was make her more aggravated.

Layne silently left him be, going into her small office and shutting the door to find some privacy inside her own house, where she could focus on anything other than the past twenty-four hours.

CHAPTER EIGHT

The next few weeks were inarguably painful from Layne's perspective. If there was anything that made her top ten list of things she hated, it was having a bodyguard hovering over her day and night. There was no opportunity to have privacy aside from hiding inside her own house.

One silver lining was that she had convinced her dad that taking away her work would result in allowing her skills to get rusty, and her contacts would have a lot of questions about where she had gone. Scott was in agreement that Layne had a valid point and reinstated her duties after two weeks off. However, she was still stuck with around-the-clock eyes on her.

The guard currently on watch was James. He was only a couple of years older than she was, but he had years of experience doing a bunch of the grunt jobs for Scott and Mick. He also had a personality that was far too serious.

They were in the back kitchen of a local pizza joint, the owner trembling as he sat in a wooden chair that threatened to snap underneath his weight. Kevin Beal, the proud proprietor of "Slices of Heaven Pizzeria," had been late on a payment due to one Scott O'Reilly. Let's just say that her family did not appreciate not getting what was owed to them in a timely manner.

Layne was standing in front of him, eyes analyzing the look on his face. James hung back by the door with a grumpy expression on his face but was ready to spring into action if needed. God, the way he hovered though, it was so damn distracting.

"You know, Kevin, my heart bleeds for you. It totally does. These are tough times." Layne gave him a pouty frown that insinuated she was sympathetic to his troubles. Her hand pulled out a baby Glock from the back of her snugly fitted black pants and casually held it in her hand just so he could see where this was going.

His eyes widened at the sight of her firearm. "I swear, I can get the money next week. Please, just give me a chance." His pleas were pathetic. Did this guy have zero backbone?

Layne looked back at James who hadn't changed the expression on his face for the past ten minutes. "He sounds like he regrets not having our payment ready on time. What do you think?"

James didn't so much as blink at her. What a damn killjoy. Layne shook her head and turned her attention back to Kevin. She stepped closer to him, crouched down in front of him, resting one hand on his knee while she casually waved the semi-automatic pistol around as she spoke.

"Next week doesn't help us when the money was due this week. But, I tell you what, I like you, Kevin. You make really shitty pizza, but I like you. You get the money to us next week, and for our troubles, go ahead and double it. Deal?" Layne was in strict business mode as her eyes stared at Kevin's face which had several lines of sweat coming down it.

He was very quick to nod, "Y-Yeah, that's a deal. I promise I will have the money. Ok? I swear."

Layne stood up and leaned over, pecking a quick kiss on his cheek. "That makes me so happy to hear. Thank you, Kevin. It's a date for next week." She backed up and turned to approach James, before recalling she had one more thing to add. Turning to look back at Kevin who had just been filled with relief, "Oh, and just so you remember this time." She aimed the Glock and fired a single round at his leg. The sound of the shot echoed against the walls of the tiny kitchen.

The poor sap screamed out as the bullet entered his thigh, his hands grabbing onto it. Layne looked to James and patted him on the arm. "Let's go." She tucked the Glock back into the back of her pants, making sure her shirt draped over it to keep it concealed.

They left the pizza place, walking out onto the street into broad daylight. Layne flinched at the sun shining so harshly today. Slipping some shades over her eyes she looked up at James who was at her side, barely giving her space to breathe. "Can you at least pretend like you're trying to give me space?" Her brow arched questioningly, but James just shook his head.

"No." That was all he had to say. He was a man of many words it appeared. She sighed. This was just painful dealing with an unnecessary and unwanted protector. Pulling out her secured cellphone, she made a brief call to Liam letting him know that Kevin would be paying them double next week and had been incentivized to keep his word. That was the last of the business matters she had on her plate for the day. She walked with James back to the car where he drove her back to her house.

Trying to think of a way to strike up a conversation he would actually engage in, Layne sat in the passenger seat, opening a bag of dill pickle-flavored potato chips. Crunching into the first one was utter bliss.

Working always stirred up an appetite for her. "You want one?" She extended the bag to James while he kept a watch on the road like a hawk.

"No, thank you." His voice was flat and monotone.

Layne shrugged and continued to snack on the chips, basking in the tangy and salty flavor.

"Aren't you bored of this whole gig? I would be." He didn't respond to her, leaving them in more awkward silence. She decided that if he was going to be as dull as a Fisher-Price butter knife, then it presented a challenge for her to overcome.

"For shits and giggles, what would happen if I happened to ditch you? On a scale of one to dead, how much trouble would you be in?"

James glanced over at her, before averting his eyes back

onto the road and resigning himself to the small talk. "It would depend on if anything happened to you and how long before we tracked you back down."

"So, let me take a guess. If I get hurt on your watch, you're basically a dead man walking? If you only happened to lose track of me for a short period of time, you would be less dead?" Layne sucked the potato chip flavor off her pointer finger.

"Depends on the type of day your father was having."

Layne gave a little chuckle. "Ain't that the damn truth. The moody son of a bitch."

James cracked a subtle smile, but she caught it out of the corner of her eye. "So, you do have a personality somewhere in there. Good to know."

After they both arrived back at her safe haven and settled inside, James still didn't leave. It had been weeks of this bullshit and she was getting sick and tired of it to the point of considering straight-up violence just to put an end to the nonsense. He took a seat in her living room and began to read a magazine.

"I'm going upstairs to try and catch a quick nap. Feel free to help yourself to whatever food is in the fridge." Layne jogged up the stairs, walking down the hall to the master bedroom. She shut the door behind her, stripped her jacket off, and flung it onto the bed.

From behind, a gloved hand clamped down over her mouth to stifle any screams. Layne instinctively went for the gun still tucked in the waistline of her pants. Her attacker's free hand snatched her wrist and twisted her arm behind her, limiting her movements.

"Shhh," a husky voice hushed into her ear. Seamlessly, as he spun her around, he disarmed her of her pistol while releasing her. Layne was ready to lunge at the intruder until she saw a very familiar sight. He had on the same black tactical attire and the same black skull mask concealing his face that she had seen down at the docks weeks ago.

Her muscles relaxed as she recognized it was Joey, her heart rate slowly recovering. She approached him, expectantly holding out her hand palm face up.

"My gun." She kept her voice quiet so James didn't hear anything from downstairs.

Joey gave a playful grin, feeling proud of himself. "You promise not to shoot me?"

"You will just have to take your chances. Right now, you're looking at a fifty/fifty shot."

"Ouch, I would have thought it would have been at least forty/sixty."

"You should be so lucky." She waited until he finally passed it back to her. Layne walked over to her dresser, ensured her Glock was unloaded and no longer live, and laid the weapon right on top to be cleaned later. "What are you doing here?"

"You're a hard woman to get alone these days."

Wasn't that the damn truth? "I'm working on that."

He followed her over to her dresser and plucked a bright pink thong that was hanging out of the top drawer. "I didn't peg you for a fan of the color pink."

Layne pulled the panties off his finger and flung them back into the drawer, shutting it tightly.

Joey suddenly went quiet, shifting his stance in a way

that was unnerving to her. She looked over at him while she took her hair tie out of the ponytail it had been in all day, allowing her dark hair to drop down behind her shoulders.

"You haven't come back here to finish the job, have you?" Only partially teasing him.

He shook his head, but his demeanor screamed that he was all business now. "No, but I found out some information that you need to know. I don't have all the details yet, but it's not looking good."

Confused about what type of information he could have she crossed her arms in front of her chest. "Usually any information in our line of work isn't good. What is it?"

Joey stepped up to her, his hands gently sliding up onto her arms, "The 227 project I asked you about at the docks. It's you. You're the project."

He wasn't making any sense, and it prompted her to wrinkle her brows together and shake her head. "That doesn't make any sense, I have never even heard about it. I would know if I was working on something."

He corrected her. "No, Layne, it's about disposing of you."

Downplaying the scenario, she shrugged. "I pissed someone off, what else is new?" She had heard all these things before. All it took was one whisper to get the criminal rumor mill lit up in a frenzy.

Frustrated, he let out a short sigh at how little she was taking seriously. "Layne, you're not listening to me. This isn't a Franzetti project, we don't know where it is coming from. Initially, we thought that you were working on something that was going to be a massive blow to the Franzetti family, that's why Michael needed answers to see what you knew. But that's not the case, Layne."

"As much as I would love to give Michael a run for his money, I'm not that stupid." It had been a long day and Layne couldn't wrap her brain around what Joey was telling her. It didn't even make sense. Sure, she had been increasing her footprint in the organization, but she still wasn't making the big decisions in the family.

Why would she be considered a big enough threat to anybody? As a pawn, she could see that scenario, and as a target to leverage that would even make sense, but what he was insinuating didn't.

"Your intel is wrong, Joey. That doesn't even make sense."

"My sources are always right, don't you just brush this off as nothing."

Layne stepped back from him as she battled all the feelings inside of her right now, trying to come to terms with whether he was telling the truth and what if he was right. What did that truly mean for her?

"I will take it under advisement. You need to leave before someone realizes you're here." After their last encounter, he had made it clear he wasn't going to play the role of Prince Charming and be her gallant knight, not that she wanted him to.

The puppy dog brown eyes of his had a softer look than normal in them. "I'm not going to leave and put you at risk."

"That's funny coming from you. Look, you can't—" starting to have raised her voice she caught herself and lowered it again, "—you can't stay here. Looking all," she waved her hand around to wildly motion at his attire, "like this. It's creepy as shit."

He tilted his head and leaned in closer to her. "You didn't seem to mind it down at the docks."

She chuckled. "You and I have two very different recollections of what went on that night."

His gloved hands latched onto her hips as he pulled her up against him. "I could tell by the look in your eyes." One hand slid behind her onto her lower back and then settled onto one side of her ass. "It's the same look you have in your eyes right now. I bet you're just dying to be a good girl for me, Layney."

She inhaled sharply trying not to lose her train of thought as his touch caused electrifying reactions deep inside of her body. If he kept talking like that, her legs were going to melt into a puddle on the floor. Looking up at him, her hands slid up over his sculpted biceps. "I told you not to call me that."

"I'm going to call you whatever I want, and you're going to like it."

Lightly she bit her lower lip, her body craving more of him like a sexual designer drug. "I thought you weren't a knight in shining armor?"

"I'm not. I told you, you get a one-time deal."

"In that case." Her hand dropped down to feel over the front of his crotch, rubbing over the sizeable erection that strained against the zipper of his pants. "We are going to compromise. You take me out on a proper date, and then you get one night of me being a *very* good girl for you. How's that sound?"

As her hand fondled him, his cock throbbed and Joey groaned in excitement. "How do you propose that I do that with your little entourage?" His hand took hold of her wrist to keep her hand right where it was.

Layne smiled up at him and tugged down the front of his mask briefly just enough to expose those perfect lips, she gave them the lightest of kisses. "You're smart, you'll figure out a way." Her hand gave two pats to his chest reassuringly and slipped her hand out of his hold.

He took a moment to adjust himself in his pants before walking over to the bedroom window that overlooked the back patio. He stared at her with a thirst in his eyes. "Be careful, Layne. Don't get yourself into any more trouble."

She couldn't help but smirk when he said that. "I think trouble has already found me, and if trouble doesn't get the hell out of here, he's going to risk causing an all-out war. Go." Her hand shooed him to leave.

He left, and Layne flopped onto her bed wondering what the hell was wrong with her. She was putting so many aspects of her life at risk, for what? A one-time fling with a dick that already had her charged up and ready to go?

Before she could honestly answer that question, she felt something underneath her vibrate and buzz. Confusion set in, and she reached underneath her, feeling an item that was thin and hard in her back pocket. When she pulled it free, she took a look at the phone that didn't belong to her. The screen lit up with a text message from an unknown number.

UNKNOWN

Be ready for me Friday night at 5:30.

I'm never late.

That sneaky bastard had managed to leave her with a clean and secured phone. She smiled to herself, impressed that he had successfully distracted her enough to slide it into her back pocket.

CHAPTER NINE

The week had crawled by at a snail's pace. The more Layne attempted not to think about her and Joey's official outing on Friday, the more it kept creeping into her mind at the most inconvenient times.

It was Friday morning, and she had purposely made sure her work schedule was cleared for the latter half of the day. She had told Joey that he was going to have to figure out a way they could get together even with eyes constantly on her, and she wasn't sure that he was going to be able to pull off a plan.

When she had texted him throughout the week, she hadn't received any return messages. Being left out of the loop and not having details was a pet peeve of hers. Call her crazy, but she liked to have a solid plan in advance for everything and anything. She was a bit of a control freak like that. How was she even supposed to know what attire to pick out if she didn't know what the plan was?

With the lack of communication from him, she had her

doubts as to whether or not he would even show. Worst case, he stood her up and she found a quick date at a corner bar to spend the night with. She wasn't going to let some bad news guy chase her back home into pajamas and a pint of ice cream, all because he didn't know a good thing when he saw it.

That thought spiraled into an even worse worst-case scenario, what if this was all a setup and he was just going to deliver her head on a silver platter to Franzetti? Cue the paranoia. That's why she was going to be prepared with safety measures. One could never be too careful these days, especially if somehow, they were going to ditch the body-guard of the day, Lenny.

She unwrapped the piping hot curling iron from her dark chestnut strands and watched as the last section of hair was freed and bounced into a loose curl. Layne stood there in front of the bathroom mirror analyzing what she saw in her reflection.

Her outfit was one of her more casual looks, but she figured he wasn't an uptown trust-fund baby expecting her to pull out the finest threads for this little get-together. Her favorite pair of dark blue skinny jeans flattered the shape of her legs and fed into her favorite pair of thigh-high black boots with laces up the back. For a top she had opted for something that screamed innocent and flirty, a white cropped blouse with thin straps that criss-crossed over her back, leaving her flat stomach exposed. To polish it all off, she grabbed a black jacket so that her favorite pew-pew could remain concealed in the back waistline of her pants.

Glancing at the smartwatch on her wrist, it was 5:02

p.m. Seeing how quickly the half-hour mark was approaching, a series of figuratively squirmy butterflies bounced inside of her stomach. It had been a long time since she could recall getting this worked up over a date, and not just any date, a date that she wasn't even sure was going to happen.

A knock came at her bedroom door which had been left open. Layne left the bathroom to see who was at the door, color her disappointed that it was Lenny standing there.

"Just got a call from Liam, he wants to debrief you on a situation."

Talk about shit timing. "Right now?"

Lenny nodded. "Said it was critical."

The irritation and frustration set in. "Crap, okay. I will be down in a minute."

The tall and lanky guard left without another word to return downstairs. This was going to be such a letdown after going through all the effort to dress herself up for this.

"Liam with the perfect fucking timing," she muttered quietly to herself as she snatched the phone Joey had left her and tucked it into her pocket so she could text him in the car to cancel.

By 5:07 p.m., she was sitting in the back of the town car and Lenny was pulling away from the front of her house to bring her to midtown to meet up with Liam on whatever it was that he decided was so incredibly urgent to discuss. Retrieving the phone from her jacket pocket her fingers tapped away at the screen to give Joey the bad news.

5:11 P.M.

LAYNE

Got called to a meeting, on my way there now. Not looking good for tonight.

5:12 P.M.
UNKNOWN NUMBER

I'm never late.

Well, kudos to him for being punctual, but she was stuck in traffic heading towards midtown. Layne sighed and leaned back in her seat, staring out the window. She was going to be royally pissed off if this debriefing ended up being a waste of time.

Lenny cursed at the other cars also sitting in the traffic, occasionally laying on the horn to make his displeasure loud and clear.

Another text came in on the phone at 5:29 p.m.

UNKNOWN NUMBER

Better be ready.

Staring at the screen of the phone, she found herself questioning if she had been clear in the prior messages to him. He did realize she wasn't even home, right?

"Oh, you son of a bitch! You could have gone through that light!" Lenny yelled from the driver's seat, waving his hand around angrily during his fit of road rage. The offense? The car in front of them stopped at a yellow traffic light.

Layne's eyes looked at the clock on the front dash which ticked over from 5:29 p.m. to 5:30 p.m. "Never late, my ass."

Lenny looked up into the rearview mirror at her. "What was that?"

She shook her head. "Nothing."

The purr of a sports bike drew closer, moving in and out of the stopped cars on the avenue. A bike rolled up right next to Layne's passenger side door, the rider putting his feet on the ground to steady the ride between his legs.

When she noticed the biker stopped right there, she raised a brow questioningly at the odd decision to come to a stop on the marked dashes between the lanes. The man on the bike turned his head to look over at her while he sat there. That's when she saw on the black helmet, white decals designed into a skull mouth on the front of it. There was a spare helmet right behind him on the back of the seat.

"What the hell is this asshole doing?" Lenny had noticed the bike situated there on the dashed lines dividing the lanes. Layne grinned like a giddy schoolgirl and seized the moment.

She swung open her passenger side door and hopped out. Not wasting any time, she pulled the helmet down over her head and mounted the back of the sports bike, scooting herself close to the man's back as she wrapped her arms around his waist.

"Shit!" Lenny exclaimed as he scrambled to get out of the car and run around the front as Layne made her exit.

The bike's engine revved several times before taking off, accelerating down between the cluster of vehicles. He maneuvered it through the intersection expertly to avoid getting taken out by oncoming traffic.

Lenny got left behind at the car, running his hands

through his hair as he realized that he just somehow managed to lose the boss's daughter. He kicked a front tire. "Damnit!" Even if he had gotten back in the car, there was no way he would have been able to get through the congestion and catch up with the stranger Layne took off with.

He got back into the car, immediately making the phone call to Scott to alert him of the situation.

"Hi, sir. I—" he cleared his throat to muster up the balls to admit what he had allowed to happen on his watch, "—I, have some news about Layne. She took off with some guy on a crotch rocket."

After the initial escape, Joey drove at a more reasonable speed. He didn't take the time to tell her where they were going, but she noticed that they were going over the Brooklyn Bridge right as the sun was dipping down below the horizon.

Layne kept herself securely situated on the back of the motorcycle. There wasn't much talking to be done while they were traveling. At least not verbal communication anyway. While it couldn't be seen underneath her full coverage helmet, she smiled mischievously as one hand slid down to Joey's upper thigh, giving it a firm squeeze. Her thumb stroked over the inside of his leg suggestively as her hand glided up over his zipper to the top of his pants.

His body tensed as Layne's touch continued, feeling her fingers slip under the front of his shirt and begin to travel south inside the front of his pants, but before she could execute her bright idea, he moved her hand back up to the front of his flexed stomach.

It seemed someone didn't like being distracted. She

chuckled in light entertainment and behaved herself as she watched all the sights around them pass by.

It was incredibly liberating to know that she had successfully ditched her security detail. They may not have known it, but she knew that Joey was far more capable of keeping her safe than the recruits who worked trying to make a name for themselves in the O'Reilly family operations.

CHAPTER TEN

Finally, they eased to a stop and the engine cut off. When Layne looked past Joey's shoulder, she saw a narrow and battered boardwalk separating them from a sandy beach where the water was lapping at the shore.

He stepped off the bike and removed his helmet. Layne remained there on the back seat, taking off her complimentary head protection.

"Oh good, it really is you. I was concerned that maybe I had just hitched a ride with some random guy." She smirked as she set the helmet down on the seat between her legs.

Joey held out a hand for her to take, assisting her off the back of the bike. Layne didn't decline in taking the assistance.

"And if it had been a stranger, he would have been one lucky son of a bitch with the way you were providing quite the distraction."

"You're welcome." She winked at him.

"C'mon." He kept a hold of her hand and led her towards the quiet and unoccupied beach.

It was a welcome reprieve from the constant noise pollution of Manhattan. Joey released her hand so he could hide both his hands in his pockets as he stared at the last bit of sun reflecting off the water as it sunk lower in the sky.

"It's not much, but I like to come here when things get too heavy."

She stopped right next to him, linking her arm through his. "I can see why. It's like a mini-escape from reality."

Layne rested her head against the side of his arm as her eyes drank in the scenery of the ripples of the water caressing the shoreline. She could have stood there with him, getting lost in the serenity of this spot for days. What she really should have been thinking about was the chain reaction of events her taking off was going to cause, but instead, she found herself wondering why she had never felt this level of ease with any other man.

When she eventually took her eyes off the mesmerizing waters and looked up at Joey, she was surprised to see him looking right back at her. Turning to face her, his finger gently moved underneath her chin and tilted it upwards. Her breaths seized in her chest in anticipation as his mouth approached her rose-stained lips.

Layne pressed an index finger to his lips before they were able to connect with hers, giving him a sweet smile.

"Sir, our date has only just started. What kind of girl do you think I am?" Joey eased her finger away from his mouth, drawing it to the side.

"You're going to be in so much trouble later." The glimmer in his eyes showed he had every intention of following through on that. He dropped his finger from underneath her chin and took a peek at the time showing on a silver watch on his wrist. "If we don't get going, we are going to be late."

"Late for what?"

"For someone who comes off like she knows everything, you ask a lot of questions. Just trust me, eh?" He led her back to his bike, but instead of mounting it, he walked right on by.

It was several minutes of walking along the sidewalk before they arrived at their destination, a cozy brick building with no discernable signage indicating if it was a business or residence. Once he escorted her in through the front door, it was clear it was a homey little restaurant. There were not very many tables in there, and the ones that were appeared to barely fit in the room.

"Are you sure they're open?" Layne noticed there wasn't a single soul to be seen.

"For us they are." Joey grinned at her with a mischievous wink. His fingers slipped between hers as he took them into the kitchen, where it was clear they were no longer by themselves.

An elderly woman stood in front of the commercial stove, stirring a metal pot of red sauce with a wooden spoon. She was a frail-looking thing, but what she lacked in height and bulk she made up for in an aura of warmth and kindness. Her soft blue eyes were set behind a pair of thick glasses that were a little too large for her face and her pure white hair was kept in short but voluminous soft curls. The well-aged woman banged the wooden spoon on the edge of the pot to rid it of excess sauce before setting it down on a ceramic spoon rest.

"Ah! You made it, finally." She wiped her hands off on the front of the vintage-looking apron wrapped around the floral fabric of her dress. The woman turned and gave them both a larger-than-life smile.

Approaching Joey, she reached out her wrinkled hands and cupped his face. Her hands had a minor shake to them that one could venture came naturally with age. She pulled Joey's face down and greeted him with a kiss on each cheek.

Then, she turned to Layne, still emitting an extraordinary level of happiness despite being strangers to one another. "So, this is the one, huh? What a beautiful young lady!"

Layne was surprised to then be welcomed so affectionately by the woman when she released Joey and embraced her in a warm hug. It reminded Layne how long it had been since she felt such a motherly gesture. Layne gave a light squeeze back to the woman and smiled sweetly. "Thank you."

Joey spoke up, "Layne, this is Marie, but everyone calls her Nonna."

Marie nodded in agreement. "Everyone who comes through that door is family here. Especially this one right here." She hooked a thumb at Joey. "Now, the sauce is on the stove." She wagged her finger at Joey. "And don't you go messing it up by adding anything else to it now. It is absolutely perfect the way it is." Her words were firm with him, though not nearly as threatening as they should have sounded.

Joey's finger crossed over his chest. "Cross my heart."

"Mm-hmm." She eyed him skeptically. "You two have fun," she stated as she pulled her apron off and hung it up on a hook near a narrow set of stairs that led to an upstairs apartment.

After Marie retired upstairs, Joey removed his leather jacket, hanging it up next to Marie's well-used apron. He went to work setting up a pot of water on the stove.

Layne watched, unclear of what to do with herself. It wasn't often she found herself in a kitchen with someone else. "Do you need help?"

"You can help by taking a seat right there." He pointed at a stool by a center island where he set two plates down.

She tried to reassure him of her competence. "Believe it or not, I can reasonably find my way around a kitchen."

"Sit your pretty little ass down, Layne."

"Yes, sir." She stripped off her jacket, adding it next to Joey's before taking her assigned seat.

He continued to work his way around the spotless kitchen, preparing them a meal complete with freshly made garlic bread, a side salad, and a dish prepared with al dente spaghetti covered with Nonna's sauce and meatballs. All made with love. The final touch was the two wine glasses filled with a rich chianti wine.

"I didn't take you for the type to cook for a girl or..." she examined the label on the bottle of wine. "Know your wines."

He settled onto the stool next to her. "I didn't take you for the type to be so easily impressed." Joey smirked at her as he took a sip from his glass of wine.

They both chit-chatted over the meal. Talking about everything from his upbringing to her time out west. Layne felt like she could have eaten five more pounds of the meatballs alone they had been so delicious. Joey's hand rested on top of her thigh while he listened to her speak.

"Rebecca is my best friend, but she doesn't get my life, not truly anyway. She's been around long enough to know enough about how dangerous it is, but not how far down the rabbit hole it goes. Some days it's a relief that she is in the dark about it, and other days…" Layne's voice trailed off, leaving the thought incomplete. She shook her head and finished off her glass of wine. "Now it's your turn, Mr. Big and Bad. How is it that you got into this life?"

"I'm not sure there's enough wine for all of that." He chuckled, pouring Layne another serving before topping off his own.

"My mom got locked up when I was young, busted on drug charges. When she got out, instead of thinking about seeing her kid, she went straight to her dealer to get high. The cops found her with the needle still stuck in her arm in an alley. My old man barely knew I existed except when his bottle was empty and needed a refill." He gave a shrug of his shoulders as though it was a story that had been spoken a hundred times.

"Nonna has been the only one who ever showed she gave a shit since I was a kid. She made sure I never went hungry, she tried to make sure I stayed out of trouble, but I had a mind of my own there. Got sent to Rikers a few times, met a few guys who showed me a few things, and here I am." It sounded like such a simple explanation, but there was far more to it than that.

Joey had come to terms with his life never having been happy-go-lucky and had even embraced it so that he was comfortable with the man he had become as a result of the unfortunate circumstances.

She listened to how rough his upbringing had been in comparison to her own. Layne didn't have it all easy though, pain and death had been splattered across her life like an arterial spray. "And what about the whole mask thing? Is that just some kinky shit that gets you all ramped up when you go in for a kill?"

"No, but I think it gets you ramped up though." His hand squeezed her thigh suggestively before sliding to the top of it, inching up closer to her center, seemingly going to repay her for her distraction on the ride here.

She bit her lower lip in response to his touch. "You didn't answer the question."

"I will answer it if you answer mine."

Layne shook her head. "That's not how this works, but fine, I will play."

"The morning after we met, were you thinking about me while you were touching yourself in the shower?" His fingers brushed over the crotch of her jeans, prompting her cheeks to burn red hot and her hips to twitch in excitement.

So, he had been in her house long enough to overhear her pleasuring herself after that vividly hot dream she had. Layne should have been embarrassed and perhaps even mad about the invasion of her privacy, but she wasn't.

"Maybe you should have come up there and joined me instead of lurking." Her hand drifted between her legs to meet his, intertwining her fingers with his and guiding him away from her aching core.

He smirked as she could see him imagining what could have transpired if he had. "Now who's not answering the question?"

"It's a first date, a girl has to keep some secrets."

"In that case, we have one more stop to make." Joey winked at her as he rose from his seat, pulling her up out of her seat onto her feet with him.

After they both cleaned up their dishes so as not to leave Nonna a mess, they retrieved their belongings, and Joey guided her outside.

"What's next in your playbook?" Playfully she grinned at him, wondering what other tricks he was going to pull out of his bag for the rest of their time together. He struck her as the type of guy that always had a plan.

"I had to ditch my playbook for you. I didn't think you'd go for the flowers and a five-star restaurant."

The smile on her face hadn't faltered since they left Nonna's. "You're not wrong."

He led them back to the sports bike they arrived on, handing the spare helmet over to her. "One last stop." Layne pulled the bulky helmet on and got on the bike behind him making sure she was scooted all the way up against his firm backside.

They took off, the headlight on the front of the bike cutting through the dark of the open road ahead of them now that evening had fully descended on the city. The cool air whipping around them made her grateful for his body providing a shield against it and giving off some residual heat.

When he turned the engine off in front of an older apartment building, it was hard to fully see its historical charm at this time of night. It only rose to maybe seven floors tall, a short building by New York's standards. The reddish-brown bricks looked mismatched as if they had replacements throughout the years resulting in uneven fading. The street lights reflected off the glass entryway doors. A callbox mounted to the right of the doors was only one of a few features that gave away an indication of more modern amenities.

Joey helped Layne off the back of the bike, taking both helmets and locking them in place onto the bike. Leading her by the hand, he took her inside the double set of doors and to the elevator. Once they were in the confined space of the metal box, he stood behind her resting his hands on her hips. The button for the seventh floor was lit up as their destination.

"Lucky number seven, hm? Seems fitting." She observed.

"Why's that?" His mouth was closer to her ear than she had realized when the warmth of his voice fell against her neck.

She leaned into him, her ass teasingly pushing back

against him as her hand reached out to pull the bright red stop switch on the elevator's control panel. They were roughly five floors up when the car ceased its movement between floors.

Layne twirled around to look at him face-to-face, not hesitating to pull herself up to the front of his chest, her lips crashing onto his. All her needs funneling into that passionate moment full of heat and desire.

Joey's hand came to hold onto her face while the other drew her even nearer at her lower back. The searing kiss intensified as their bodies pressed into one another. He guided her back until she was up against the wall. She was unable to escape the feeling of the strength of his hard body on her—in every regard.

Layne devoured his taste, consuming all of it and willing to drown her very soul in it. After fantasizing about this night after night, she was now getting exactly what she had been pining for.

Even when she should have come up for air, she couldn't bring herself to do it. She couldn't tell whose breath was in either of their airways. Joey's mouth was the most addictive drug she had ever experienced. His tongue possessively claimed hers inside of her mouth while her figure rubbed up against him in a suggestive fashion.

His hand slid onto the top of her breast, roughly kneading it in his hand, indicating she hadn't been the only one thinking about this moment. Her pert nipples were poking at the light fabric of her crop top in a delighted reaction to his touch.

Assertively she pushed him back to the wall opposite

her with a smile on her face, breathless. "We're going to need more time than this elevator is going to stay held up for."

Joey's hand gave a smack to the red stop switch, popping the button back in, causing a jolt of the lift as it continued its ascension once more.

As far as she was concerned, she had an itch, and Joey was the only one that was going to be able to scratch it. Her hand reached out and grabbed him by the belt of his pants, pulling him back towards her. He responded by nipping at her throat, hungrily speaking with the deep gravel of his voice rumbling against her skin. "Hope you cleared your schedule. I'm going to take my damn sweet time enjoying all of you."

The doors opened and she backed up out of the elevator, already in the process of unlatching his belt. Feverishly she captured his lips again while he fumbled for the keys to his apartment. Layne spoke between breaths and sporadic kisses. "I'd be disappointed if you didn't. I hate being disappointed." Her playful smirk promised an array of all the sinful delights ahead of them.

Joey reached behind her as they came to unit 701, twisting his key in the lock and swinging the door open as he prepared to begin the ravaging.

Layne shrugged off her jacket, tossing it to the floor as they both stumbled inside. Using his foot, Joey kicked the door shut directly behind them. The unit was blanketed in darkness, causing them to bump into a side table knocking some unopened mail onto the floor.

The clearing of a throat interrupted what should have

been nothing but silence in the apartment. The light in the living area flickered on. Joey and Layne weren't the only ones there in that apartment.

CHAPTER ELEVEN

It took a moment for Layne's eyes to adjust when the darkness in the apartment was cast away by the sudden light. Standing there in the living room were two men, one of whom she would recognize any day of the week; Michael Franzetti.

The thinning raven hair was long enough to pull into a small bob of a ponytail. A patchy goatee on his face, and one of those flesh-colored moles on the side of his nose the size of a shirt button. He was dressed in a gaudy-looking suit with a mixture of patterns and colors that were abrasive to the eyes.

Shit. That was the first thought that fired off inside Layne's head.

Standing next to Michael was a heaping giant of a man, whom she didn't recognize, with a scowl on his face. Layne could only assume that he was hired muscle to keep Franzetti safe and protected.

It was challenging to get a good read of Franzetti's expression, if he was surprised to see Layne there with Joey it was well concealed. The strap of her top hung off the side of her shoulder. Layne immediately pulled it back up into its place as she swallowed down her anxieties while trying to process the gravity of the situation that had just presented itself.

On the other hand, Joey's demeanor immediately went ice cold, his hands casually relatched the belt of his pants as though they hadn't been about to be yanked off just a few seconds ago.

"Go home, Layne." Joey sternly told her.

"Ah, ah, ah. The evening is still early, and the party has only just begun. Take a seat." Franzetti motioned to one of several open spots to sit there in the living room.

Layne glanced at Joey, looking for any indication of his thoughts on the next action he was going to take, but he didn't take his eyes off Franzetti. She stood there silently begging for some signal they were on the same page here.

"SIT!" Michael roared like a petulant and impatient child as he showed signs of running out of patience. The sudden outburst caused her to flinch.

Getting any closer to Franzetti wasn't anywhere on her top ten list of things she wanted to do, ever. Layne ran a quick calculation and risk assessment in her mind. Normally, her fight-or-flight instincts erred towards fighting. This was one time she knew that staying not only put herself at risk but her family and everyone else who worked for the O'Reillys.

She pivoted on her heel and ran to the door, flung it

open, and dashed out as Joey had originally told her to do. Bursting into a sprint down the hall towards the fire exit stairwell, she glanced behind her to see if Joey was going to follow.

Crash.

Layne collided with another ape of a man built solidly and towering over her. His arms locked around her like a vise, lifting her off her feet and easily carrying her back to apartment number 701. She bucked, trying to break his hold on her at least enough to get her arms free.

"Let go, asshole!"

She was taken right back into the apartment, and now Joey stood in front of Franzetti in mid-conversation in the living room. His attention was drawn from his employer to Layne being brought back into the apartment.

"I told you; she doesn't know shit. Just let her go run back to daddy."

The hulkbeast of a man restraining her didn't loosen up his hold until he flung Layne like a ragdoll onto the sofa with enough force to cause it to rock back and bang against the wall. The momentum and movement of her body caused her gun to unknowingly slide out from the back of her pants, sinking between the cushions.

Franzetti stood there, holding his hands together in front of him. "See, that's the dilemma. Is it that she really doesn't know anything, or are you just letting your dick do all the thinking for you? I would like to think I'm a good judge of character. All I'm going to do is ask her a few questions."

A vein popped up in the side of Joey's neck as his blood pressure rose.

Layne sat up on the couch, murderously glaring at the man who had tossed her there. Michael approached her, sitting on the edge of the coffee table in front of her, his arms resting on top of his knees as he tried to come off as friendly and approachable. She knew better. He was about as friendly as a pissed-off hornet nest.

"Layne, I would like to think that we have mutual respect for one another, given our lines of work. Call it professional courtesy."

She shifted her gaze onto Michael's scumbag face, the glare not altering one bit. Keeping her mouth shut she waited for him to get to his point of what he wanted.

"All this buzz about this 227 project just isn't going away, and I feel like I wasn't invited to the party. That hurts my feelings."

"Boo-fucking-hoo, that makes two of us. You're operating off of bad intel." She finally spoke up, unsympathetic to his concerns.

Franzetti sighed. "Such a fresh mouth on such a beautiful face." He looked back over his shoulder at Joey while chuckling in twisted amusement. "I can see the appeal."

He looked back at Layne. "I really would like to believe you, dear. Yet, you've managed to compromise one of my best contractors here with your wits and charm. Let's make a deal that benefits everybody." He reached out to place a hand on her knee, his thumb stroking the inside of it.

"If it doesn't involve putting a hole between your beady eyes, I'm not interested." Layne shoved his hand off her.

He took the hint and kept his hands to himself but leaned over, dropping his voice down to a whisper. "Just wait until your poor father hears about all of this. I need to know if you're telling the truth, so you will just have to forgive me." Without any hesitation, he snatched a handful of her hair, yanking her up onto her feet as he stood.

Joey lunged, only to be pulled back by the two hired hands as he yelled out viciously. "You touch her and I will fucking kill you!" One of the men slammed a fist into Joey's stomach in an effort to subdue him, causing him to double over.

Michael dragged Layne out of the living room, harshly yanking on her shiny chestnut locks close to the roots. He took her into the glaringly bright white bathroom located down the hall where the tub was pre-filled with water. The bastard had planned on someone taking a swim tonight.

"I dislike getting my hands dirty Layne, but having the opportunity to dish some karma back at Scott O'Reilly… Mm, it's just too good of an opportunity to pass up. Now is your last chance to be a helpful little flower."

Her fingers scratched and pried at Michael's hand tangled in her hair, beginning to solidly plant her feet into the ground upon seeing the still and eerily calm body of water in front of her.

"Go to hell."

Franzetti smiled, seemingly delighted that she chose noncompliance. He kicked the back of her knees, causing them to buckle under her. Layne's body fell into a kneel in front of the tub and as she yelled out, he shoved her forward over the edge of the tub plunging her head into the cold water.

It was a shock to her system as the air disappeared around her. Layne's hands pushed and shoved against the edge of the tub while her feet scrambled to push herself up. Franzetti's other hand pinned her down against her back with his weight against her.

She tried not to panic, but the struggle of her body was quickly diminishing what little air she had left in her lungs. Just when she thought that she was nearly out of oxygen, he pulled her head back up. An involuntarily loud gasp as she drew in much-needed air came out of her mouth. Her heart was beating so hard that she was pretty sure it was about to burst through her chest walls.

Michael leaned down to the side of her face, giving her an emotionless look. "The 227 project?"

"I don't kn—" and before she could complete her response, he thrust her head back under the surface of the water. Being a little more prepared for it this go around only helped marginally. Water was splashing out of the tub onto the floor and the walls. Once again, she felt the slow depletion of life in her lungs before being greeted by the cool air in the bathroom as she was drawn back up again.

"Last chance, sweetheart."

Her lungs were on fire as she sucked in heaps of air. "I… I swear, if Joey doesn't kill you, I will."

"Unlikely. Say hello to your mother for me." He pressed his slimy lips to her temple.

This time when he shoved her back down into the tub, he used all his weight to keep her under, minimizing the amount of flailing about she was able to do. With all the water getting splashed on the floor, her feet were slipping against the tiles. Her hands scratched at the smooth sides of the tub for anything to grab onto. It seemed like hours with her head fully submersed, and everything began to feel light as a floating sensation took over her senses.

She remembered the smell of her mom's homemade chocolate chip cookies.

She could feel her mom's loving embrace and the light fragrance of peonies in her perfume.

She could hear her dad's voice and see the beaming smile on his face as he told her how proud he was of her when she stood up to the bullies on the playground.

She could hear Uncle Mick's laughter as Liam and she tackled him to the ground during a snowball fight.

She could feel a heat deep inside aflame as Joey looked into her eyes and how he had kissed her like she was the only woman on the planet.

That was the last thought she had. Joey had been her last thought.

Franzetti left Layne's soaked body, void of any movement, slumped over the edge of the tub. The strands of her hair were in a wet and tangled mess.

He grabbed a hand towel off the rack, wiping his hands dry as he came back out into the living room to see that his two right-hand men were taking turns pitching shots at Joey. He gestured to them both, prompting them to drop Joey onto the floor in a heap. Michael stood there feeling tall and mighty as he tossed the damp hand towel down onto Joey.

"I'm going to make myself crystal clear. The only reason you're not dead is because of all the work you have done for me in the past. Let this be a lesson to you that if you ever fuck up a job this badly again, I won't be nearly as kind."

Joey groaned as the back of his hand wiped some blood from his mouth, struggling to get up on all fours. Franzetti turned to leave, then paused. "Send my condolences to her family for me, will you?" The asshole even made an attempt at sounding half-sincere when he said it before he left with his two goons.

As for Joey, the realization of the words Michael parted with sparked a surge of adrenaline. He scrambled onto his feet and ran to the other side of the apartment, through his bedroom, and into the master bath. His heart sank into his stomach at the sight of Layne's body hanging there over the side of the tub.

His body moved before his mind could catch up, in an instant he was pulling her back to lay her down on the floor. "Layne! Layne! Wake up!"

His hands checked her over frantically, cupping her face and shaking it hoping she would just awaken and open those mesmerizing green eyes. Joey brushed her hair away from her face, "Fuck, no, no, no." Coupling his hands one on top of the other, he began chest compressions on her. His arms locked and steady as he stared down at the peaceful-looking Layne lying there on his bathroom floor.

"You stubborn bitch, c'mon!" He shouted at her in frustration with each compression that felt useless and ineffective. "Layney, please. Please, Layney." His voice cracked with raw emotion.

She sputtered up the first wet cough, followed by several more as she expelled water out through her nose and mouth. He rolled her onto her side quickly to ease the coughing fits as she gasped a few times. Layne groaned as her entire chest, inside and out, felt like she had been run over by a freight train, twice. Slowly she sat herself up, Joey's hands assisting.

"Take it easy." He stared at her, relief overwhelming him as she gazed up at him with those entrancing doe eyes he had fallen for the very first day they met.

Joey's hands held her face. Overwhelmed with gratitude that she escaped death's cold grasp, he kissed her with gentle affection. Her hand ran over the side of his face as she weakly returned his kiss as she tried to gather her wits.

Drawing away slightly, she winced as her entire body screamed at her in pain.

With a light rasp to her voice, she offered up a light curve of a smile. "Ten out of ten do not recommend drowning." Layne went to chuckle, but immediately whimpered and rubbed a hand against her chest at the fresh round of aches and pains. Joey kissed her forehead with a sigh. "You have no idea how much you had me worried."

As she tried to get up onto her feet, Joey shook his head. "Oh, no you don't." He scooped her up into his arms, holding her securely to the front of his chest. Normally, she would have protested at being carried anywhere, but he felt warm and safe. Not to mention she wasn't confident her legs would have had the strength in them.

Layne rested her head against his chest, closing her eyes and focusing on how the air felt, moving freely in and out of her lungs. He carried her out of the bathroom and over to the edge of his bed where he sat her down.

"Stay here." Joey left and returned with a dry towel, wrapping it around her. His hands rubbed her arms to help dry her off and generate warmth through her body.

Layne should have been feeling an unholy rage inside of her toward Franzetti, but instead, all she could do was keep looking at Joey in awe that she wasn't robbed of ever seeing him again.

"I should have had things handled, but-"

"Shh." He pressed a tattooed finger to her mouth to stop her right there. "We aren't doing this. We aren't doing the blame game. What is going to happen is you are staying here tonight. I'm not letting you out of my sight. Everything else will get dealt with tomorrow."

She let out a quiet sigh as she gently moved his finger away from her lips. "I'm okay, Joey. Really. I don't need to stay here."

"It's not up for debate, so shut that gorgeous mouth and deal. I will go get you some dry clothes."

Her energy was entirely spent after the evening, and arguing with him was looking less and less like a priority. Allowing Joey to get the final say this time, she let him take care of her just this once. One time couldn't hurt anything.

After getting her his old Slipknot t-shirt, he gave her privacy to change while he walked around his apartment securing every possible entry. He came back into the room to see that the size of the shirt swallowed her up. Even in that oversized shirt, she made it look hot as hell.

He got Layne tucked into his bed, lying next to her until she fell asleep. His hand rubbed up and down her back soothingly while he studied each of the features of her face. Joey vowed that he was never going to let anyone try and take her from him again, he couldn't let that happen.

CHAPTER TWELVE

Morning rolled around and Layne rolled right into Joey's side as she began to feel her slumber fade away. Half-asleep, she curled up against him and draped an arm over the smoothness of his bare stomach. He lay there on his back, shirtless with the top sheet loosely draped over his lower half.

Protectively, Joey drew his arm around her shoulders, pulling her in even closer. When she opened her eyes and lifted her head to take a look at him, his soft brown eyes were already open and staring at her.

The tattoos inked across his skin were now on full display before her. Various designs and images sprawled in a sleeve over his left arm, onto the back of his shoulder out of sight, across his toned chest with one-offs branching off down his ribs and up his neck. Of the splashing of multiple images across his skin's canvas that stood out the most, she saw various scenes of bloody skulls and roses, birds, and the words 'Chaos Addict.'

Joey smiled in amusement; his other arm tucked behind his head. "Good morning."

Layne cracked a smile. "What's so funny?"

He shook his head. "Nothing."

"Tell me!" She gave a shove to his side, prompting a laugh from him.

"You have the cutest little snores I've ever heard."

"I don't snore!" She propped herself up on one arm, hoping it would help solidify her defense.

"Whatever you say. I know what I heard."

Her eyes looked him over, becoming suddenly aware of his lack of clothes. Layne appreciated the sight of each of the muscles on display in front of her like a heavenly buffet. Joey didn't interrupt her as her eyes drank in the view, but he did pull her up on top of him.

Her legs spread to straddle over his hips as she got comfortable in the new position, her hands resting on top of the chest she had just been admiring seconds ago. He reached up and tucked a section of her hair back behind her ear. "You know, this is not what I expected for your first time spending the night with me."

Layne tilted her head. "Oh?"

"I imagined a lot less clothes." His smirk oozed with charm.

Leaning over onto her forearms as she sat atop of him. "Don't worry, you wouldn't have gotten that lucky last night."

"I find that very hard to believe by the way you were trying to climb me in the elevator."

She smirked back at him and rubbed herself teasingly

over his hips where she could already feel the growth of his morning wood pressed up against her, begging for attention. "I don't give it up on the first date, too many bad apples to waste the effort on."

His hands latched onto her hips as he pulled her down harder against him with a groan of approval. "Good thing I'm counting this morning as our second date."

"Mmm." Layne bit her lower lip as the sensation of grinding against him had her panties soaked with her own arousal.

Her hands slid down over the tanned skin of his stomach, fighting every urge inside of her to just give in. Leaning down onto him, she lightly kissed his lips, feeling the stubble around his mouth scratch at her face with a bit of a tickle.

"I don't give it up on the second date either, but a third date? That might be the charm." The glimmer of playfulness shone in her green eyes.

Joey rolled over, pinning her underneath him as his hand slid to the front of her panties. The hem gave away as his fingers invited themselves into the poor excuse for a layer of clothing. His fingers found her excitedly wet clit, stroking it with slow intentional movements. Layne whimpered as her legs spread enough to allow his hand to go to work between them.

"Such a good girl, already all wet for me. You want to revise your stance on waiting for a third date?" His finger circled her nub again, causing her to bite back a moan at the sensation. Layne pulled her upper half up to him, burying her face in the side of his neck to muffle the sweet sounds he was causing her to make.

The sounds she made against his skin only encouraged him further as she squirmed beneath him, her hand clenching onto the sheets underneath her.

"What was that, Layney? I didn't get that." He smirked as he pinched her wet little button.

Her voice was heavy with desire as she looked up at him as his fingers relentlessly teased her sensitive bundle of nerves. "I can't think when you do that."

Joey knowingly grinned as his fingers continued to explore and tease her body. "All you have to do is say it, Layney. Tell me you want it."

He slid a finger down her slit and pressed it inside of her to drive his point home. He leaned down, his stubbly cheek scratching against her neck as he gave it a nip followed by a press of his lips against the sensitive skin. "I will fuck this tight pussy of yours until you scream loud enough for the entire damn city to hear."

Her hands gripped onto him desperately, one burying into his shortly cropped hair while the other clutched onto his back, her nails digging into his flesh.

Layne's hips pushed against that one finger sliding in and out of her. God, she needed him more than life itself at that moment. She had been telling herself since the moment she had laid eyes on him that he was bad news, and maybe she was right, but damn it all to hell if she didn't care right now.

"God, Joey, please…" her breathy voice was laced with wanton disregard for anything but him.

He looked at her with a devilish grin. "That's my good girl." He didn't hesitate to crush his mouth to hers, claiming it with the eagerness of a starving hellhound. His hands were quick to get to work on yanking her panties off. Their mouths explored one another, sparking an electrifying sensation throughout Layne's entire body.

With a hand on the back of her neck, he sat back, pulling her upright. "I need to see all of you." His hands stripped his well-worn t-shirt off her, revealing the supple curves of her bare breasts. Carelessly, the shirt was tossed aside to join her thong on the other side of the room.

Layne dropped her hands onto his sides as she sat there fully exposed to him. She gave a small grin as his eyes lit up. "You see something you like?" She watched as his eyes slowly roamed and appreciated every detail of her body.

"I'm never going to let anyone else ever touch you again like I'm about to. You're fuckin' stunning, and every part of you is going to be all mine." He pulled off his black boxer briefs, exposing his long and thick length which was fully engaged and ready.

Layne was glad that her three-inch assessment in McGregor's was far off base. On a scale of one to ten for Layne, by comparison to any other man she had been with, Joey was so far off the charts he was halfway to Mars.

Her hand didn't hesitate to reach out and wrap around his massively hard cock while she looked up at him with a need and desire unlike anything else she had felt in her lifetime. As she stroked him, it elicited a groan of approval from Joey.

He guided her back down onto her back. "Uh-ah,

there's going to be plenty of time for that. Right now, I'm dying to taste you." There was something alit in his eyes that made her stomach fill with glorious anticipation. It then magnified when he firmly took her by her wrists and pinned them above her head with one hand easily. She squirmed against his hold, the feeling of helplessness and vulnerability prompted even more excitement from her body.

His mouth came down onto one of her breasts, taking one of her stiff nipples hostage, sucking on it nice and slow. She arched her back, pushing her breast further up against him. His hand, which wasn't forcing her to keep her hands to herself, latched onto Layne's other breast. A delightful whimper escaped her as he ran his tongue around the tip of her nipple before his teeth gave a teasing nibble to it.

After getting a taste of both of her bountiful breasts, he released her wrists so he could run his hand down along the front of her body where both hands settled on her hips. His lips traveled their way down her stomach, journeying lower inch by inch. The further down her body he got, the more she felt like her desire was going to explode.

Layne dropped her hands down from above her head to get her fingers lost in his hair. He slid down to right above her center, the strength of his hands now rubbing over her skin from her hips over onto her inner thighs. His hands grabbed her thighs as if he owned them and spread her legs wide to fully expose the sight of her pussy that was throbbing and aching for his attention.

"Layney, you're already making a mess of the sheets with how wet you are. I bet you're just aching for me to bury my cock in you." His mouth hovered over her inner thigh, his tongue escaping and drawing a long line over her skin.

Feeling the warmth of his breath against her body, her hips rocked forward, trying to make contact with his mouth, but he made sure to stay just out of reach. With a yearning in her eyes, she looked down at him. "I want it. I want all of it. Your mouth, your hands, your cock." She pushed her hips forward again, still not getting what she wanted as she made a small sound of frustration.

Joey smirked at her, enjoying seeing her struggle without control. "Such an eager little girl. Don't worry, you're going to get all of me."

Without another word, his tongue gave one long lap against her slit causing a jolt from her body as she moaned out at first contact. Joey savored the taste of her body, already becoming a slave to how addictive she was going to be for him.

His mouth captured her now highly-sensitive clit, sucking intently on it. Asserting his control over her body, his hands held her by her thighs as she wriggled underneath him while the strokes of pleasure zipped through her body like lightning.

Her hands squeezed tightly onto his head as she cried out, feeling a quick and furious escalation deep within her. With every sound she made, it prompted him to take more of her and explore all the sweet tastes of her pussy.

Just when she thought her body couldn't take much more and it teetered on the edge of falling into the depths of ecstasy, he pulled back and looked at her mischievously.

His tongue ran over his lips, gathering the remnants of her most intimate flavor from them. "Did I tell you to come yet?"

With her climax having been so damn close and now receding from the edge it had been so close to spilling over, she whined in desperation. "Joey, please, I was so close. That felt so good, I need more of you."

"You didn't answer my question, Layney." He let go of her thighs and moved up higher on her, meeting her mouth with his. The taste of her arousal still lingered on his tongue as a reminder of how he had used it to bring her to the edge of release. The head of his shaft teased against her opening as he briefly lost himself in the taste of her mouth before pulling back.

"I want the first time you come for me to be all over my cock while screaming my name. You're going to be a good girl and do that for me, aren't you Layney?" His words made it clear he was in total control of the situation in his bed. It wasn't like her to let a man call the shots. But, for Joey? She already knew that she didn't want anything else but to have him take full control over her.

She nodded in response to his question. He could have asked her to rob a bank, and she would have done it. It had made her nearly lose her mind, feeling the tip of his shaft so close and he still hadn't given it to her. Her hand reached down, attempting to coax him to push himself a little closer to her opening, but he promptly removed her hand, pressing it down into the mattress at her side.

His fingers grabbed her face. "Don't be a brat, I will give it to you when I think you deserve it."

"I need to feel all of you inside me." Layne was used to getting what she wanted, and it was clear that Joey wasn't going to let that fly. "Fuck my brains out, Joey. Take all of me."

He sat back and flipped her onto her stomach, pinning her upper body down while propping her ass up in the air, drawing a gasp of surprise from her. "Oh, that was always in the cards. I just need to hear you say one more thing for me." His hips were up against her ass, the tip of his erection teasing as it rubbed against the tight entrance to her sex.

"Tell me you're mine, only mine."

Feeling a primal heat overcoming her, her hands balled up the sheets. "I swear, I'll be a good girl. I'm all yours."

Hearing her promising to be a good girl and give herself to him, Joey growled as he sank himself deep inside of her in one smooth push. Layne's body forcibly stretched and wrapped around him as she moaned out as a mixture of sensations swam over her. A little bit of pain and a whole lot of pleasure as her tightness was forced to accommodate him. Her hips pushed back against him as she felt herself filled with the hard length of his shaft.

"Fuck, Layney, you're so goddamn tight." His hands ran down the length of her back and over the curves of her ass where he squeezed them while he drew himself back before pumping back into her again. Joey took his time, enjoying each languid movement inside of her.

Layne's heart was pounding inside of her chest as she maintained her position on her knees with her chest pushed down onto the mattress. It felt akin to being a lioness in heat while the king of the jungle claimed her body. Repeatedly. Over and over again. Nothing else could have made her feel more alive than being there in his bed with him driving himself into her.

As his tip stroked over her body's deepest sensitive spot, she felt a trembling threatening to take hold of her. Barely being able to catch her breath as her sexual high drew nearer, she clawed at the headboard in front of her, tensing up her entire body.

Joey groaned, feeling her bear down around him. "That's it. You're taking my cock like such a good girl. Now, fuckin' come for me, Layney." His words were strained between each of his thrusts as his own swell of pleasure was drawing closer to its peak.

Hearing both his praise and his demand triggered her vision to explode into stars as her release violently took control, and her body was wracked with ecstasy. She screamed out his name as her climax rushed over every part of her from head to toe.

Joey didn't slow his movements, eliciting a steady stream of pleasurable cries from her, extending the high he had given her while the inside of her pussy spasmed around him.

The next thing she knew as the fog in her head cleared, he had paused briefly to turn her onto her back where she was staring up into the depths of his brown eyes as he held himself over her.

Each of his muscles flexed while his hips mercilessly pushed himself back into the wet mess of her cunt. "I'm not done with you yet," he said while his hand held onto the side of her face, his thumb trailing down over her bottom lip.

Layne was in such a haze from her first orgasm that she could have died an extraordinarily happy death right then and there. Lightly she sucked on the tip of his thumb as it passed by her mouth. "Mm, you have me feeling so good right now, you could do anything you want with me."

A sinful smirk crossed his face. "Don't tempt me more than I already am." His face closed the gap between them, capturing her mouth with his own as he continued to build a second swell of warm pleasure within her. Her fingernails dragged across his upper back, her hips meeting his as their bodies repeatedly joined together.

His movements were getting less and less smooth as he groaned out while trying to keep a grasp on his self-control. She wrapped her legs around his waist, locking them at her ankles. Her body felt so conflicted as her back arched pushing her up against him trying to escape the intensity of feelings that were quick to build back up once more and craving another dive off the precipice of divine release.

"You're gonna make me come again." Her words were forced out through her panting and heavy breaths. No sooner than she said it, the orgasm ricocheted throughout her. Layne screamed out, clutching onto everything and anything within her reach. Her fingernails left scratches along his back.

Joey's body stiffened as he rammed himself as deep inside of her as she would take him, holding himself still as he gave a feral groan. The throbbing of his cock finally maxed out as his sticky seed erupted into her depths before he collapsed down on top of her into a sweaty pile of entangled body parts.

Thank God for birth control.

Layne's head was swimming in a glow of hormones and emotions that she had no business feeling. She kissed the top of his head as he basked in his own post-release euphoria.

"Fuck," she muttered still in a state of absolute bliss. "That was worth breaking all of my rules for." She'd had her share of decent one-night stands, but this one topped the charts.

He lazily lifted his head up off her chest with a satisfied smile. "Just wait until round two." He pulled her face in for an affectionate kiss as he rolled them both over so that Layne ended up back on top of him. His dick still felt quite at home inside of her.

"What makes you think you'll be lucky enough?" Her head rested on top of his chest, while she listened to the thudding of his heart.

His hand playfully came smacking down on her ass cheek. "Call it intuition."

"Well, Mr. Intuition, you're going to have to wait. I have to get back home and see what hell has broken loose since I ditched Lenny yesterday."

It was a sobering thought that she had to go back to reality and likely some highly pissed-off people, particularly Liam and her dad. Though, it was worth it. So incredibly worth it.

CHAPTER THIRTEEN

Despite her protests, Joey was adamant that he bring her back home. After the incident with Franzetti, there was a whole new level of complication in Layne's life. He made sure to leave her a few doors down where they exchanged goodbyes.

"Thanks for everything," she wanted to avoid any awkward discussions with him and leave things in a good spot between them. "Take care of yourself."

All the talk back in his apartment during their morning romp she chalked up to mere words in the searing heat of the moment. Neither of them needed any long-term entanglements, not when they both led very chaotic lives.

She stepped away from the sports bike before he could try to say words they would both regret, and half jogged up to the steps leading up to her home.

He sat watching her until she reached her front door and then took off. The sound of the exhaust fading the further away he got.

After letting herself inside, when the door shut behind her, she had captured the attention of several unexpected house guests; a few associates who worked for the O'Reilly family, Uncle Mick, and Liam who was paused halfway down the stairs.

Everybody was staring at her and the silence was deafening. It was her Uncle Mick who spoke the first words. "Thank Jesus, Joseph, and Mary." He let out an exhale like he had been holding his breath for hours before coming over to her and pulling her into the biggest of bear hugs. Layne blinked a few times and gave a small squeeze in return.

"Um, hi. What is everyone doing here?"

Liam came down the steps, if he had been relieved to see her it wasn't obvious given the level of heated emotions rolling through him. "What the hell, Layne?"

Mick released her but stayed nearby in case a mediator was required between her and her sibling. Her brother looked like he was barely holding onto the last straw of restraint he had ever been given. "Tell me what the fuck happened!"

She held her hands up in front of her defensively. "Whoa, calm down. Look, I ditched the babysitting patrol, I take full responsibility for that, but that's all because you couldn't keep out of my business. But this," she gestured to the number of people currently standing around her home looking through her belongings, "this is excessively overreacting!"

"Overreacting?" Liam's voice raised another decibel. He pulled his phone from his pocket, shoving it into her hands. "How else do you think we should be reacting when we get this note from Franzetti, huh, Layne? What the fuck happened?"

She fumbled with the phone that was thrust into her palm. Turning it right side up, she saw a photograph of a bouquet of white roses and a note attached to them that read, 'Condolences on the loss of your daughter. -M.F.'

Layne winced a bit, there wasn't a whole lot she could do to smooth this one over.

"I need answers, Layne!" Liam's barking voice startled her slightly as she tried to figure out the best way to give him an explanation. He snatched the phone right back out of her hand. "You know what this did to dad? I'm surprised the man didn't have a fuckin' stroke!"

She ran her fingers through her hair taking a deep breath in. "It's complicated, Liam."

"Un-fucking-complicate it!"

Mick stepped forward, lightly placing a hand on Liam's chest to try to get him to ease up. "Alright, let's all just take a moment here. Layne is alive, and someone should let your father know as much before he outright wages a war on everyone in the entire damn state."

Layne shook her head, guilt starting to weigh on her about how the situation escalated beyond even what she had anticipated for a rebellious night out.

"Look, I went on a date. It was a fluke that I ran into Franzetti, one thing led to another, and he may have tried to drown me. But look," she motioned to herself, "I'm fine." Sure, she was understating the turn of events last night, but just like anyone else there, she didn't want a war breaking loose.

"Goddamnit!" Liam turned and violently crashed his fist into the nearest wall.

Mick turned to look at Layne, rubbing the side of her arm. "Let's get you back to headquarters so we can straighten this all out. You know your dad is going to need more than the Cliff's Notes version, Layne." She knew that he was absolutely right about that.

Everyone wrapped up what they were doing, and Liam refused to utter another word to her. She got into the passenger's side of Mick's vehicle where it was just the two of them. He looked over at her empathetically. "You want a piece of advice?"

"You're going to give it anyway, you always do."

He nodded. "That's true. Well, here's my advice; be honest. We can't help if we don't have all the facts."

She leaned back in the seat, glancing up at the roof of the car, and shook her head. "You know, I always appreciate your advice, right? Ever since I can remember, you've always been the best shoulder to lean on when things seemed unbearable. But this? It's different."

Mick frowned, mulling over her response before he reached over and patted her leg. "It may seem that way, but whatever it is that has you spiraling, Layne? You're more levelheaded than this. Whoever the guy is, he's not worth it. He *will* get you killed."

She looked over at him, furrowing her eyebrows as he pinpointed it down to being a guy issue.

"I'm smarter than I look." He flashed a smile at her as he pulled away from the curb.

Joey was going to get her killed. She couldn't exactly argue that given she barely survived last night.

When they arrived at O'Reilly Manor, she was led into Scott's office where Liam was already seated in one of the two chairs positioned across from the glossy mahogany desk their dad sat behind.

"Sit," was all Scott had to say to her. There was no grand family reunion and rejoicing she was alive. No emotion was present at all in his voice, just a simple one-word command.

Today was not the day she was going to push buttons, so she went ahead and situated herself in the vacant seat.

He only gave a brief look to his son. "Liam, you can go."

From the change of Liam's face, he had expected to be a part of this conversation and wasn't pleased that he was being excluded. But, like the good little soldier, he up and left, slamming the door shut behind him for extra measure on how he felt about it.

Now that it was just the two of them there in his office, Layne almost wished that Liam had stayed. Almost. The tension and unspoken awkwardness in the air was stifling. Her dad peered at her from across his desk, his hands lightly folded in front of him.

"I thought I lost you like I lost your mother. Do you understand what level of excruciating pain that has been? I don't know what the hell happened, Layne, but I need to know. And, so help me, if you lie to me about any of it."

Each time she thought of a way to start off her explanation, it never seemed to be the right thing to say, so she sat there for a solid five minutes under the weight of her dad's gaze as he waited patiently for her.

"I know I messed up. I met someone, and apparently, he has a history with Franzetti. It was all a series of bad coincidences. Franzetti is going on a bender about some project he's heard about in the grapevine, and when I didn't have the answers, he got doubly ticked off."

Her father leaned forward as this was all news to him. "What project?"

"Some project 227, that's all I know." She shook her head.

"227?" He repeated the number back to her.

Layne nodded, affirming he had heard correctly. "He thinks it's something we're doing that impacts him, but I have a source saying otherwise."

"We don't have anything we are working on with that name, Layne. He's barking up the wrong tree."

"I know that, but…" she hesitated to even say anything further given the sensitive nature of it and what her dad's reaction potentially would be.

"But, what?" Her dad prompted her to continue.

"My source said the project is about me. I mean, it's not clear how, but that's all the info I was able to get."

It was one of the few times she ever saw her dad get taken back in surprise when he wasn't expecting something.

"Who else here knows about this?"

She shook her head. "Just me."

"Let's keep it that way. Where did you get the information from?"

Her teeth lightly bit into her lower lip. "I-I can't tell you that."

"You can, and you will, Layne. I'm not going to play games here, not with something like this. If something is going on related to anything or anyone in my organization, there is going to be hell to pay. Especially, if this all turns out to be true, it will make this whole Franzetti situation look as inconsequential as an incorrect weather forecast."

"He does contract work, and Franzetti was just the last person who hired him."

"Layne, that doesn't even make sense. If he works for Mike, then why would Mike be willing to go to these lengths to determine if it has something to do with him?"

She shrugged her shoulders. "I don't know, that's why I didn't say anything because I'm not even sure it's good intel."

Scott stood up and circled his desk so he was standing in front of Layne, taking her hands, and easing her up out of her seat. "I will get to the bottom of this. Until I do, this chaotic behavior has to stop. You don't talk to anyone having anything to do with Franzetti. He's already going to be livid you made a fool out of him by not actually dying. You got it?"

She nodded in agreement. "Got it."

"Second, for appearance's sake, all your jobs are going to be reassigned for now. Once we sort this all out, things will go back to the way they were."

"And the security detail?" Call it wishful thinking, but

she had hoped that she would get a response different than she knew it was likely to be.

"I will tell them to give you a little more space, but I'm not calling them off entirely. If you try to ditch them again, I will lock you away in a tower and throw away the key."

While he may have only been joking about the tower, it wouldn't be far off from what lengths he would go to if it was to keep her safe. Layne felt it was at least a fair compromise, and she wasn't going to push back on it.

"And, one more thing," he drew in a steadying breath as he pulled her in against his chest and kissed the top of her head. "Don't ever give me a scare like that again. Understand?"

Layne hugged her dad back, nodding against his dress shirt during the rare moment he showed any emotion at all. Scott held her for a few moments, refusing to let her go before he was ready.

"What are you going to do about Franzetti?" She lifted her head to look up at her father, curious how he was going to handle this political shitshow of an attempt to snuff out her life.

"I have a few connections that are telling me that there's someone who is particularly adept at handling sensitive situations like this and looking for new work."

She raised a brow, curious enough to want more information and potentially be involved. If they were going to make a move on Michael Franzetti, she wanted her sweet revenge. After all, she was the one who had almost been drowned here.

"You have to let me get involved."

Her dad immediately released her and shook his head. "No, absolutely not, Layne. That's not an option."

"I'm the one he tried to kill, Dad! I should get my chance to serve him up a big dose of karma."

"We hire specialists for jobs like this, it needs white glove treatment - not emotionally driven revenge."

She rolled her eyes in annoyance as she crossed her arms in front of her chest. "Getting drowned is pretty fuckin' emotional."

"And we didn't see it coming. Franzetti is smart, and he's already prepared for the shit to hit the fan." Scott rubbed her arms reassuringly to try and persuade her that this was the best course of action.

"Please, dad. Let me at least vet the specialist, let me have some hand in it. I think I deserve that much."

Contemplating the minor ask, her dad finally gave in. "Alright, but you listen when I tell you to back off."

"I promise, I will." She criss-crossed her finger over her heart.

"I'm serious, Layne. When I tell you to leave it alone, you have to leave it alone."

"I told you, I promise I will back off if things get out of hand." She tried to reassure him by offering up a sweet-as-pie smile and giving his hands a light squeeze. Something told her that he wasn't thoroughly convinced. Hell, she wasn't even fully convinced she could just let this go.

CHAPTER FOURTEEN

Things didn't progress as quickly as she would have preferred. A few weeks had gone by, and she found herself attempting not to think about Joey and their one night together. The exceedingly great parts of when they had been together, and then the not-so-good parts such as the whole brush-with-death thing.

He had made it clear when they first met that he was the one-and-done type, and she was comfortable with that. Layne didn't need attachments and complex relationships in her already complicated life. The phone he had given her ended up shoved into the bottom of a drawer until its battery ran out of juice.

As much as it irked her, she had been doing her best to avoid work at her dad's request and to tolerate the security detail that was still hanging around. Only this time, instead of them hanging out inside her house, they generally stuck to exterior watches. Nobody came or went without them knowing, and if she went somewhere, they followed in a separate vehicle versus needing to be attached at her hip.

Scott had been working to put the word out there that he required a specialist who could handle the very delicate Franzetti situation. So far, everything had been radio silent.

Word on the street was that Franzetti had blown a gasket when he realized that Layne hadn't actually drowned. There was nothing like bruising the man's ego that he couldn't even do a job right himself.

It was a mild autumn day, and since she had nothing better to do than be an uptown girl, she spent the morning on her back patio curled up in a cushy chair reading a book. The story itself was nothing but pure smut, making it difficult to keep her mind clear of anything related to one delectable Joey De Luca. Out of frustration, she closed the book and tossed it onto the small glass table in front of her.

What else was a poor little rich girl supposed to do with her day when it didn't involve beat-downs, debt collections, and illegal bookkeeping? She picked up her cell from the seat next to her and scrolled through until she brought up her favorite contacts. One name in particular; Rebecca.

Her bestie since childhood, Rebecca was probably the only one who tolerated Layne's idiosyncrasies and lifestyle choices when it came to the family business. She lived a much more clean-cut life, and Layne lived vicariously through her when she needed to imagine an escape from her current insanity.

She selected the call button and waited for the familiar voice on the other end to pick up.

"Girl! It's about damn time you called!" Rebecca's perky voice was a ray of sunshine on the other end of the line. It brought forth a smile from Layne and immediately lifted her mood. However, she could tell from the background noise on the other end of the line that Rebecca was still in Cancun soaking up the sun and tequila. Lots of tequila.

"I know, sorry, it's been an eventful few weeks." Layne quietly sighed, and yet even with all the music and drunken shenanigans happening around Rebecca, she still managed to pick up on the tone Layne used when she was stressing over things.

"Oh, no. Alright, spill it. Do I need to hop on a plane right now and beat the crap out of someone? Well, do I need to tell you to beat the crap out of someone? You're much better at it than I am." Rebecca giggled on the other end of the line while a series of cheers of "Shots! Shots! Shots! Shots!" raged on in the background.

"No, nothing like that. It's just forced downtime, and you know how well I do with that. My dad throws me some extra cash and expects me to happily go spend it on Fifth Avenue like it's therapy."

Her friend scoffed. "It *is* therapy. I've told you, I will make the sacrifice and go spend the money for you any time you need."

Layne grinned and made a mental note to at least snag a new pair of ridiculously expensive designer workout leggings for Rebecca this week so when she returned, they both could hit spin class together with fabulous-looking asses.

"You're right, as usual. I won't keep you from all the fun any longer. I just needed to feel a bit more grounded."

"That's my job, I will see you when I get back and we will have a girl's night and catch up, okay?"

Layne agreed and they said their goodbyes. The talk was everything she needed to get a kick in the ass to go and do something like a normal twenty-something-year-old. She gathered her things and was out the door less than thirty minutes later.

She drove down to the fashion district where she could waste her time hopping from store to store. A few of the clerks at the concierge desks at several stores recognized her and were sure to give her the VIP treatment, champagne and all. If there was one thing that Layne knew about high-end shopping it was that champagne never hurt.

Selecting a few items to try on, she headed back to the dressing room while her assigned security guard stuck to his post right outside the store's front entrance.

She finished off the flute of champagne as she stepped into the excessively large fitting room. It was large enough to be considered a bedroom by comparison to places like Old Navy or Macy's. In the center of the square-shaped room was a round pedestal with mirrors coming from all angles on the walls to ensure one could give themselves a complete visual inspection.

Layne peeled away her shirt, exposing the black lace racerback bra she had on underneath. Before she could slip on one of the three tops she had gathered, there was a knock on the door of the dressing room.

"Thank God, this is going to need more champagne."

She muttered quietly to herself. When she opened the door, instead of it being the female sales associate she had been working with, it was a familiar face that she hadn't realized how much she missed.

"Joey?" She blinked a few times as he slipped into the room with her. His gaze slowly looked over her as his hands slid onto her hips. Before he could attempt to dial up the charm, she stepped back and snatched one of the shirts from a hanger.

Layne may have missed him, but she sure as hell didn't miss the fact that they were supposed to be a short and hot fling. He was supposed to go back to his life and she hers.

"Don't get dressed on account of me," he slyly remarked.

She shot him a slight glare as she yanked the shirt down over her head and pulled her hair out from underneath it afterward. "What are you doing here?" Then, the more she thought about it she changed her question. "How did you know I was here?"

He shrugged but gave her the space she had created for herself. "I have my methods." Joey leaned his shoulder against one of the walls casually as he kept his eyes on her with his hands tucked in his pockets.

"Fine, whatever. Why are you here then? I figured you'd be off to find your next conquest." Layne defaulted to her defensive mode when she needed to stomp down on any nagging feelings that were going to cause complications in her life.

He placed a hand over his heart. "Ouch. That's what you think of me?"

"That's what you made clear to me when you broke into my house."

"That's because," he pushed away from the wall and stepped up behind her, his hand traveling over her shoulder and up onto the side of her neck before sliding over the front of her throat, "I didn't realize how addictive you were going to be." His breath tickled over the delicate skin of her neck, while he left a steamy trail of kisses in his wake.

Not realizing how long she had been holding her breath, she slowly released it. "Knock it off."

Joey straightened. "What's the problem?"

"Nothing, I just figured you'd be elsewhere and with someone else." She looked at her reflection in the mirror, trying to gauge whether or not she liked the shirt. She was leaning towards not.

He took her arm and spun her around to face him. "It's more than that." His fingers came up to hold her chin. "Tell me what it is."

Layne tried to turn from him, but his hold on her kept her in one spot unless she wanted to choose violence. While it was still on the table, she opted to be civil for the time being. "I have obligations to my family, and you're a distraction from that."

He had the audacity to slap an amused grin on his face. "Hm, how much of a distraction?"

She let out a flustered sigh. "Joey, I don't have time for this."

"Bullshit, your boy out front is paid by the hour and daddy's credit limit is wide open. Don't make me ask twice, Layney." His tone grew impatient with her responses.

Her legs just wanted to melt from the way he called her that little pet name, and that right there was a reminder of how effective of a distraction he was.

"I need to be able to focus on my job, and with you doing work for Franzetti, that makes it a conflict of interest. I think we already learned that lesson the hard way, didn't we?" Drowning was a hard fucking lesson.

He tilted his head to the side slightly as he mulled over her response, trying to determine if she was being fully honest with him. "I'm taking care of that."

Layne wasn't fully convinced. "Oh, is that right? Well, so am I."

He dropped his hand from her chin, but still kept her close. "I haven't been able to stop thinking about you. About us." It was a rare moment of truth and honesty in Joey's thirty-seven years.

"There isn't an 'us'." Layne corrected him. She shook her head, sidestepped around him, and began to spout off one difficult truth after another.

"You're the one who said you aren't a country club and caviar guy. You're the one who said you were going to get your rocks off and then I'd never see you again."

"I know what I said. That was before."

"Before what? Hm?" She pulled the blouse up and over her head and hastily tossed it onto a hanger inside out. Her hands began digging through the rest of the clothes, searching for the shirt she had arrived in. When she looked over at Joey, he had it hanging off the tip of his finger. She reached over and snagged it from him.

"Before I realized how much—"

Layne cut him off, "—of a good fuck I was?"

Exasperated, he began to lose what little patience he was clinging to. "Damnit, Layne! Yes, but it's more than that! It's the way you look at me, even when you're pissed off. It's the way you think you own a room even when the odds are stacked against you. It's everything you do. To think that I would never get the chance to experience all that again would either drive me insane or send me into a homicidal rage."

As he explained himself, she found herself forgetting how to handle just the basics of getting her shirt on, fumbling it in her hands. Mick's words echoed in her head about being distracted, this mysterious project no one knew anything about, Franzetti's move to eliminate her, and then there were just the basic day-to-day things in her life.

When she looked up, Joey had moved closer to her and cupped her face in his hands. The warmth of his skin on her cheeks made her want to tell him she could ignore everything inside of her head.

Layne shut her eyes trying to find the words she should say and not the ones she wanted to say. "I don't do commitments, Joey. My life is too sticky for that."

His voice was gentle. "Not asking you to."

She opened her eyes back up, hoping for a little more clarity to come to her on if she should listen to her head, her heart, or her carnal desires. "You're a stubborn ass." A small chuckle passed through her lips as she fought back the smile tugging at the corners of her mouth.

His boyish grin spread across his face before capturing her mouth in a feral kiss. His hands dropped away from her face as he wrapped his muscular arms around her waist, lifting her up from her feet.

Layne's legs wrapped around his waist while her tongue intertwined with his. Joey backed Layne up against a wall as the heat between them began to simmer.

A couple of text messages dinged on her wrist. Capturing a peek at them pop up on her smartwatch, she groaned at the inconvenience of timing. Trying her best to break the seal of the kiss for more than a quick breath, Layne managed only a word or two at a time.

"I have…to leave…to get ready…for…a meeting."

His arms pulled her up against him tighter at the thought of her leaving so soon. Pulling his mouth back, he gave her a wanton gaze. "Skip it."

"It's my dad, I can't just not go."

He pressed his forehead against hers. "In that case, guess you'll owe me one."

She indulged in a few more kisses from him before regaining some self-control over her actions and dropping her legs down from around him. Once he settled her back on her feet, she slowly got her top back on.

"Come find me when you're ready to cash in that favor." Her hand lightly patted his chest, trailing her finger-tips down across his stomach as her smile lit up her face.

Layne left the privacy of the dressing room before she risked losing all her damn senses.

CHAPTER FIFTEEN

When she arrived at O'Reilly Manor later that evening, Liam walked in through the front door moments after her. Their dad had summoned them both here but hadn't disclosed the nature of what he wanted to talk about.

"Aren't you supposed to be out getting your nails done or something?" Liam quipped.

"Aren't you supposed to be out getting laid by a hoe or something?" She fired back.

"At least I'm getting some."

Layne rolled her eyes, regretting her life choices this afternoon when she could have gotten wrecked by Joey in that dressing room. She could have fired a kill shot about Liam paying to get his kicks, but she was working on self-improvement and all that crap.

Before their bickering could devolve any further, Scott calmly came down the primary staircase that led into the front foyer. He was dressed in a dark grey suit with a dress shirt in an even darker shade of grey underneath. Layne noted that he appeared to be ready for a meeting, not just with his children, but he must have been expecting to meet with someone else tonight.

"Good, you're both here. Let's have a talk."

Liam glanced over at Layne, clearly coming to the same conclusion as she had. This wasn't going to be just any typical discussion. Not saying another word, they both followed after the head of the family.

He walked past his office until he came to a door painted in the same greige as the walls. He pulled on the handle, swung the door open, and began the descent into the wine cellar down below.

Liam made sure he cut ahead of Layne, following behind their dad like a loyal puppy. She was sure to pull the door shut behind her before she took up the rear.

One would expect the wine cellar to look like something out of the French countryside, perhaps musty and reminiscent of what you might find in a medieval castle. That wasn't the case. The glass cases housed bottles upon bottles of a multitude of fine vintages. The lighting was designed to focus all the attention on the extensive collection that spanned across all four walls. In the center of the cellar was a narrow island that housed glassware underneath.

The cellar made an ideal location when one wanted isolated privacy and confidentiality. All the walls were buffered, no cameras were installed down there, and there was precisely one way in and one way out.

Scott decisively grabbed a bottle of Cabernet Franc,

easily valued at a cool grand. "I wanted to speak with you both before Liam and I go take care of some business." He selected three glasses and began to pour each of them a serving of vino.

Layne selected the glass nearest to her, taking a preliminary sip. She wasn't a huge wine snob, beer was more her drink of choice, but she could appreciate the notes and flavors dancing across her palette.

Scott continued, "As the two of you know, I've been looking for a specialist to handle the very delicate situation that we have with Franzetti. It hasn't been easy tracking down someone with both the skillset and the discretion. The last thing I want is for Franzetti to see it coming more than he already does." He paused to taste the bold flavors from his glass.

"With that said, I believe I've finally found the right person. We have a meeting with his coordinator in an hour to talk specifics, then if all goes well, we will do a final vet with the specialist next week."

"Great." Layne swirled the red liquid around in her glass. "That gives me enough time to run back home and change."

Scott looked at Layne, his expression apologetic. "It's just Liam and I going tonight, Layne."

"What? Why? I have every right to know who is going to be doing the dirty work on my behalf." Her temper began to ignite due to the fact that he was already trying to exclude her from this.

"You don't need to be put at any more risk than you already are." He attempted to explain his reasoning.

She wasn't buying it. "That's a bunch of bullshit! I should have a say in this."

Liam cleared his throat lightly. "I agree with Layne."

She paused, looking over at Liam in a bit of surprise. "Not that I'm complaining, but since when do you agree with me on anything?"

Liam shrugged. "I just think that if I were in your shoes, and I wasn't going to be taking care of business myself, I'd want to evaluate the person who is."

Layne's hand motioned at her brother. "See? Even he gets it."

With her father silently staring down into his wine glass he donned a calculating expression, taking into consideration what they both had told him. It was obvious he was hesitant to backtrack on his initial decision, but once he lifted his eyes to Layne, she knew she had won on this matter.

"If the meeting tonight goes well and we get to the final stage of the hiring process, then you can join us next week. To be clear though, if we get to next week and there is even the slightest indication that shit is going to hit the fan, you are to leave without so much as an eye roll. Got it?"

She tried to contain the smile of victory by hiding it behind taking another sip of her beverage. "Mm-hm."

He muttered under his breath. "God help me."

Scott finished off what was left in his glass. "The meeting will be at Death's Door in an hour. Liam, do what you need to prepare, and then meet me there. Do not be late." He set his glass down on the center island and left the two of them there alone.

Layne could have picked the battle about Liam going tonight to discuss the administrative minutiae, and she should have also been involved but instead, she was more concerned about who was going to be the one getting their hands dirty. It was a strategic decision to give up one less important meeting to get what she ultimately wanted.

Giddy that she was finally getting looped back into business operations again if all went well tonight, Layne was going to be chomping at the bit waiting for next week to arrive. Until then, she would have to find a way to occupy her time.

Before she stepped away from the table to leave, Liam stopped her with a hand on her elbow. "Just because I agreed with you this once, doesn't mean that you're going to be in charge of the final negotiations next week."

She turned to look at him with annoyance written all over her face, shoving his hand off her. "Say that to me after you get nearly drowned. You may be Dad's first choice when it comes to taking over operations, but it doesn't make you his favorite."

Not waiting around to see the look on his face, she jogged upstairs. Liam was left there with a scowl on his face that he had been cursed with a sister who didn't know her place in the family. He picked up his empty glass and flung it at the wall of wine bottles, causing it to break into a cluster of glass shards.

CHAPTER SIXTEEN

Still stuck on the equivalent of desk duty, Layne tried to take the time to enjoy life a little bit more. It wasn't easy, as she often lost herself in her work.

After several shopping trips, mostly to supply Rebecca with some hot finds, she grew bored of those outings. How her father had ever expected her to take on the role of a true uptown girl was insane to Layne. She needed something with a little more purpose than running up credit card statements.

The meeting Liam and her dad held with the administrative coordinator for the specialist in the lead spot for the job had gone extraordinarily well from everything she had heard. She wasn't given much in terms of details other than there was mutual interest on both sides of the transaction.

The last step was to meet the harbinger of doom himself to ensure an appropriate fit for the job at hand. If you were going to hire someone to take out a significant player in this game, you wanted to let your gut do the judging when meeting them in person.

Until then, she was stuck trying to live the life of any other twenty-five-year-old on a mandatory staycation. Her music was blaring throughout her living room, feet dancing her around the various pieces of furniture in an impromptu dance party. If only her clients could see her now, taking the time to let loose a little bit instead of being so uptight all the time.

Her hair wildly left down, the natural dark waves indicating she hadn't taken a blow dryer to them after her shower this morning.

Her phone dinged with a new notification, causing her to pause. When she grabbed the phone off its charger, she unlocked the screen to see a message waiting in one of her dating apps. A girl had particular needs from time to time, and Layne was no exception to that.

The message was from a guy she had been speaking with back and forth over a few weeks. His name was Cole, he supposedly worked as a trader for one of the top banks in the Financial District, owned a Golden Retriever puppy, and lived out on eastern Long Island. He had invited her out to his place to take a trip out on his boat several times, but she hadn't yet taken him up on anything.

COLE

Hey, beautiful. Want to save me from having dinner alone tonight?

LAYNE

Depends. What's for dessert?

COLE

Lady's choice.

She stared at the message for a few minutes while having an internal debate with herself. Layne desperately needed to get out of the house and find a distraction that wasn't online shopping.

"Fuck it," she whispered to herself as she sent a reply back in the chat.

LAYNE

Consider me your savior.

Cole was quick to send over the details of the time and place, leaving Layne wondering if her night out was going to be a major bomb or if things were going to be smooth sailing.

He had chosen a place called Annie & Cain's for dinner. It was a swanky place that a lot of the banker types frequented to toss around their excess funds. The restaurant was a little too stuffy for her likes, but she wasn't going to turn down her original plans this evening of Netflix surfing over it.

Checking the time, she had a little over two hours to get ready and head out to the Financial District where the restaurant was located. Turning her music down to a less deafening level, she poked her head into the kitchen where her guard of the week was sitting on a stool by the counter playing a color-matching game on his phone to pass the time. He had come inside to freeload some food and never left to go back out to his car.

"I'm going out for dinner."

He perked up, immediately straightening in his seat. "Where?"

"Annie & Cain's in two hours, it's in the Financial District off of Pearl Street."

Her security guard seemed to think he had a say in this as he sat there thinking it over. "I guess that's okay."

"I wasn't asking permission." Layne may have been under watchful eyes these days, but she sure as hell wasn't under any disillusion that her status in the O'Reilly family hierarchy had changed. The chain of command still operated as it had been, with her still only being outranked by a small handful of people. Those people were essentially family, and she had no desire to try and challenge those ranks.

Her new security detail was evidently annoyed as he abruptly locked his phone and pocketed it. "Do you want me to get the car ready, or are you going to insist on making me follow you down to the subway?"

It seemed her social life was going to be an inconvenience to him, or maybe it was because he still had to take orders from a woman as long as it didn't contradict what her father expected out of him.

"You keep that attitude up I may just go on a five-mile run in Central Park tomorrow morning." Layne gave the light warning she could make his job here even more painful than he already found it. She knew damn well that this man couldn't run fifty yards, let alone five miles. With that parting comment, she left him to go get herself ready for a night out.

It didn't take long for Layne to get ready for the dinner outing. She straightened out her hair so it wasn't a wild wavy wreck, opted for a smoky evening look for her makeup, and a tiny dark purple dress that clung to her curves and had a sexy little cut up the right leg. Layne slipped her feet into a pair of silver strappy heels.

Thanks to some rush hour traffic and her bodyguard's foul mood, she arrived about ten minutes late to Annie & Cain's. Her security detail followed her inside the high-class restaurant and opted to stand off to the side near the coat room, out of sight.

The entire vibe of the inside of Annie & Cain's screamed New York's elite. There wasn't one thing in there that didn't look like it cost a small fortune, right down to the light switches.

It didn't take long before she made eye contact with Cole after she approached the host stand. As stated in his message, he was at the two-top underneath the framed black and white photo of the cross-street signs for Wall Street and Broad Street about mid-way back into the dining room. She was pleasantly surprised that he looked like his profile picture, maybe even better considering how well he could wear a suit.

When she approached the table, he immediately stood up to greet her with excitement in his eyes to see her in the flesh. "Sorry I'm late, there was construction around Central Park."

"Don't worry about it, I'm not in a rush to go anywhere. Not to mention," his eyes soaked in the sight of her, "you're worth the wait. Just, wow, I knew you were gorgeous, but this..." He took a longer gander at her from head to toe, giving a light whistle of approval and a million-dollar smile.

"Don't let the lighting fool you, I had to do a lot of magic tricks to make sure I lived up to expectations." Layne gave him a flirty wink before taking her seat across from him.

Cole was decked out in a crisp white dress shirt, left unbuttoned at the collar, no tie, and a sleek tailored black suit jacket and pants. He had the type of slender physique that said he maintained a minimal fitness routine, but it didn't scream gym rat. His Norse blonde hair expertly coifed over to one side. Everything about him screamed pretty boy, and one with excess cash to spare.

"I hope you don't mind, I ordered drinks already." As if on cue, the college-aged waitress brought over two martinis each with a corkscrew of lemon peel in them.

"You're either feeling very confident or arrogant. So, which is it?" She grinned at him as she picked up her glass and let the warmth of the cocktail coat her mouth during that initial sip.

"Perhaps, a little of both." He sat back in his chair, martini in hand while grinning like a fool ear-to-ear.

The two of them made some small talk while he ordered a charcuterie board filled with various cured meats, pickled vegetables, crackers and breads, and a variety of fine cheeses for them both to pick at occasionally while indulging in another round of martinis.

Setting her half-drank martini on the table, she smiled at him. "I'm surprised you were so persistent over the past few weeks; most guys would have just moved on to the next girl in line."

Cole didn't miss a beat, which had been a theme all evening with him. "I know what I like." He was proving to be Mr. Charming indeed.

"And, let me guess, I'm just ticking off all the boxes for you?" Layne grinned while perking up an eyebrow.

"So far." His eyes dropped to the neckline of her dress suggestively.

"Well, we'll see how many more boxes I can tick off when I get back. I just need to take care of a few things." Layne stood from her chair with a playful smile at him and left to go find the restroom.

Snagging directions from one of the waitresses, she went to the back where there were the two marked doors indicating Gents or Ladies. Before she even got the chance to step inside the ladies' room on her own accord, a firm hand grabbed onto hers and pulled her inside the New York-standard cramped restroom that was only set up with two stalls.

Layne stumbled inside and immediately found herself pushed back against the bathroom door, a gasp escaping past her lips as she came face-to-face with Joey.

She had never seen him wearing anything but casual clothing, but he must have changed things up to blend in inside the swanky restaurant. The black dress shirt fit his upper body like a glove and was tucked into an equally flattering pair of black pants. The sleeves of his shirt rolled up to his elbows, leaving his marked skin on display. This look on him had her ready to drop to her knees.

His hands were on either side of her against the door, caging her in. Something dark and brooding settled in his eyes. His hand reached down to click the lock on the door to ensure their privacy.

Momentarily she felt relief with a familiar face, but it was quickly followed by shock. "What are you doing here?"

His voice kept low, seeming to have other thoughts on his mind that ranked more than answering her question. "Keeping an eye on you, since your current guard would rather become king of Candy Crush."

Layne knew that he wasn't wrong that her current babysitter would rather be doing almost anything else but his job duties. "It's not your job to keep tabs on me."

Joey leaned in closer to her, their bodies barely touching and her back still up against the door. His hand ran down her side slowly, over the swell of her hip, and inched down towards the hem of her dress.

His eyes lingered over the visual of all her exposed skin that wasn't covered by the tight-fitted cocktail dress. "Not officially."

As his hand slid onto the bare skin of her thigh, it was then she realized she was holding her breath in anticipation.

"I'm here on a date." It was stated more for herself as a reminder than for him.

Joey gave a reserved kiss to her mouth, picking up the remnants of her martini off them. "I saw." His other hand moved away from the door and wrapped around her throat, his thumb caressing the silky skin.

Feeling the possessive hold on her, her nipples tightened and pushed against the fabric of her dress. Awareness of her own body beginning to crave his touch left Layne squirming in his hold while a chill ran over her body. "I need to get back to him."

"You will after I'm done with you." The purr of Joey's stern words made her insides tighten. His hand still holding onto her throat, his other slid up between her thighs, finding the thin strip of fabric of her thong already damp from the sight of him.

She quietly moaned at the feeling of his touch so close to her center, her hands rubbed up the front of his chest as she used him to steady herself. Her legs felt as though they were just going to drop out from underneath her. In an unexpected and aggressive yank, it didn't take much for Joey to snap the fabric of her panties and he tossed them down onto the floor.

His mouth nipped at the bottom of her ear between words. "I'm going to make sure you know how much you have been driving me crazy, Layney." The edge of a growl hung on his words before two fingers slid along her crease and pushed their way inside of her roughly.

She sucked in a sharp breath before she moaned, one hand balled up in the fabric of his shirt while the other clung to the back of his neck. Her back arched resulting in pushing her breasts against the solidness of his chest. Coated in the warmth of her arousal, Joey's fingers easily slid in and out of her with dominating movements.

His hand kept her pinned to the door by her throat while she moaned out his name repeatedly in absolute pleasure. His gaze drank in the sight of her squirming in the small space he kept her confined to. As his thumb rubbed over the already sensitive bud of her clit, Layne looked at him longingly as the waves of sensual heat grew more intense throughout her body.

"Yes, please don't stop, Joey…" The urgency of need was clear in her voice as his fingers continued to fuck her pussy. His fingers curled deep inside of her to find just the right spot to tease.

"You want to be a good girl and come for me?"

"God, yes." Her hips rolled against him.

"Tell me how bad you want it." His hand applied more pressure around her throat prompting the walls of her pussy to squeeze around his fingers.

Her body was beginning to tremble as she approached the cusp of release. "So bad." Absolute neediness filled her voice.

He then stopped his movements, his fingers buried deep inside of her, the momentum of pleasure her body had been building coming to a slow halt.

"No, please, Joey… I'm so close." Her hand dropped down to his, trying to urge him to keep going.

He smirked at her deviously. "Uh-uh. That's not how this is going to work, Layney."

She whimpered in desperation, her body needing to spill over the edge he worked her up to.

His thumb gave another circle over her delicate bundle of nerves, causing her to curse and beg for more. Her heavy breaths resulted in her breasts struggling against the neckline of her dress, which was threatening to give way.

"You're absolutely soaked right now and believe me

when I say that I want to taste every last drop of you, but," he slid his fingers out of her, raising them to his mouth where he slowly sucked the taste of her body off, one finger at a time, "this will have to do for now."

Layne swore her body was going to crumple down to the floor of the bathroom as he left her there teetering on the edge of what had been shaping up to be an explosive climax. He released his hold on her neck and smoothed out the fabric of the snug dress she had on so that everything was back to where it should have been.

"Are you fuckin' kidding me? No, come on, you can't do this." She groaned at having not gotten her firework ending stepping away from the door towards him.

"When you go back to your date, let this be a reminder of who owns your sweet cunt." He leaned in, claiming her mouth for a hot moment before unlocking the door and seeing himself out. Layne stood there with her body aching for satisfaction that only one person was going to be able to give to her, and he just left.

She took a few minutes to gather herself and freshen up, trying hard to ignore her screaming carnal desires that had been riled up to a full roar only minutes prior. When she rejoined Cole at the table, there was still a light flush on her cheeks.

Cole seemed surprised to see her back there sitting across from him. "I was beginning to think maybe you had ditched me."

"No, sorry, I got a work call that I had to take." She shifted in her seat, trying to find a new sensation of comfortable where your brain wasn't in the gutter. Her eyes glanced around to see if she could spot Joey, but if he was still lingering, he was expertly blending into the background.

Layne immediately downed what remained of her drink to attempt to wash away the sinful memories of the feel of Joey's hand nearly melting her into a useless puddle. She apologetically looked over at Cole. "I'm sorry to do this, but I have to cut our night short."

He seemed a bit taken back with slight disappointment painted over his face. "We haven't even gotten to talk about your choice of dessert yet."

She stood up, and he joined her. "I know, it's this issue at work that is going to be a problem if I don't go take care of it." Layne definitely had a problem that needed tending to, and Cole was not going to get the job done for her.

Layne said her goodbyes to Cole and rounded up her bodyguard still standing up front near the coat room. When she got a peek at his phone before he pocketed it, sure enough, she saw the brightly colored shapes of Candy Crush. Damnit, she hated that Joey was right.

CHAPTER SEVENTEEN

The establishment with the sign above it bearing the words "The Beacon" was known as Death's Door to everyone else in the criminal underground. There was a ton of speculation and urban legends on how it earned that nickname. Some people thought it was because of the eerie appearance of the exterior with its rotted door that had been the victim of one too many shoddy repairs. Others suggested it was because the clientele who frequented the joint met their fate by death more often than not. Layne's theory was that some kid probably thought it sounded cool.

The windows out front were painted over with streaks of black paint. During the day you could tell how poor of a job was done, but on a night like tonight it was effective in providing privacy from nosey outsiders. The burly-looking man standing at the door took one look at her and gave her a courteous nod, allowing her to pass him and enter the establishment. Bearing the O'Reilly name had its perks, one of which was not being questioned in seedy establishments like this one.

As soon as the door opened, she was smacked by the smell of rancid cigars, over-applied cologne, and stale booze. There would be no getting the scent out of her clothes for several washes after this. The knowledge that her dad wore his high-end suits here was mind-boggling.

Given the importance of appearances for a meeting of this caliber, Layne was sure to twist and overlap her hair into a neat braid. She opted for a pair of black pants, a hunter-green tank with a black military cut jacket, and a pair of practical and solid boots.

She also brought a girl's best accessories with her into Death's Door: a mini arsenal. There was never any telling when this level of negotiations could go poorly, and you never wanted to be stuck without the appropriate tools. Layne made sure she had at least two different knives, her baby Glock, and a spare clip.

Now that she was inside, she noted they had done some renovations and changes to the layout since she had last visited. There was a dimly lit bar in the left corner, booths lining the opposite wall, and a hall with maybe five or six doors from what she could see from where she stood.

Each of those doors led to a private room where business could be conducted. Sometimes that business was some exchange of goods, sometimes it was political games, and sometimes it was just delving into carnal pleasures. Layne shuddered at the thought of what diseases were likely left behind in such cases.

Liam stood outside the second room, flagging her down

with one raised hand. The place wasn't too busy tonight, making it easy to take the straightest path to where he was. "Is our guest of honor here yet?"

"Not yet." He held the door open to the reserved room they were going to be using for the discussions. When she stepped inside, there were two mounted lamps on the wall ahead of her using red light bulbs to provide minimal illumination. Her father was sitting in an upholstered armchair in the corner across from the doorway. Two other chairs were set up, one next to him, and one near the door.

"Layne, Liam is going to sit here." Her father motioned to the chair to his right. "And I want you standing right behind him."

She had been doing this long enough to realize he wanted her to be behind Liam not only for purposes of hierarchical structure but for safety reasons as well. Layne may not have agreed with it, but being caught arguing amongst themselves would be bad for business if anyone witnessed it.

She went ahead and leaned back against the wall behind Liam's assigned seat. Her brother remained waiting outside for this specialist her dad had searched high and low for. Her nerves were starting to tingle with anxiety while they waited.

Liam's voice spoke up from directly outside the room's entrance. "Right on time."

A tall figure appeared in the doorway, bordering just over six feet from what she could guess based on the height of the door frame. Slowly he stepped foot inside and assessed the layout of their meeting space.

Liam followed close behind and closed the door to avoid any lurking eyes or prying ears.

"Take a seat. Please." Her father gestured at the chair across from them, separated by a rickety-looking coffee table with unknown stains and gouges marring its finish.

The specialist took a few steps forward to take his seat where the lights could provide a better look at his appearance.

With her arms casually crossed in front of her chest while she remained back against the wall, the first thing she saw was the white crooked smile of the skull-faced mask. Her poker face faltered while her heart flip-flopped in her chest and knocked an entire garden of butterflies down low into her stomach. She shifted on her feet, her eyes watching as Liam crossed the room and took his seat in front of her.

Logically, Layne attempted to rationalize that just because it was a masked man didn't mean it was Joey.

He cocked his head to one side curiously. "I didn't realize this would be such a family affair."

The depths of his gravelly voice sent the hair on the back of Layne's neck up on end. She would know that voice anywhere. She knew exactly how the mouth that spoke those words would feel against her skin. Her thoughts further strayed to the heated memories of his tongue doing things to her before she had to painfully bring herself back to the present.

Joey lounged back in his chair, giving off a vibe of comfortability despite being outnumbered in this small space. His eyes met hers with a gaze that sent her reeling back into thoughts of the number he did to her at Annie &

Cain's the other night. She still hadn't recovered from how he had left her.

Scott rested his elbows on the armrests of his chair, folding his hands in front of him, "This is as much their business as it is mine. Now, before we talk terms, given the delicacy of this matter, I need assurance that you will use the utmost discretion in carrying out the task."

Joey's eyes shifted back to Scott with all seriousness. "I have a personal interest in this case, so believe me when I tell you that discretion is my top priority."

Liam chimed in. "A personal interest? That sounds like a recipe for you to get too tied up in your own shit." There Liam went, trying to insert himself into things like he was already in charge. Layne was thankful that he wouldn't catch a glimpse of the unimpressed look on her face.

This masked specialist her dad was on the verge of hiring leaned forward, perching his elbows on top of his knees while locking eyes with Liam. "C'mon over here, little boy, and let me show you what happens when someone gives me a reason to spread around some pain and suffering."

Scott shot a hard glare over at Liam the second he moved an inch in his seat. Liam slowly let out a measured count of an exhale to avoid embarrassing the family by lashing out at this guy, but the temptation had been there. Meanwhile, Layne was pushing her teeth into her tongue to prevent herself from giving even the tiniest of smirks.

When Liam didn't make a move, Joey sat back again and motioned with his gloved hand over at Layne. "So, is she the one who took a swim?" He posed the question to Scott.

Layne straightened up, stepping away from the wall she had been leaning back against. "Don't look at him, I'm standing right here."

"Sweetheart, you're not the one hiring me." Joey didn't even glance at her.

"The hell I'm not."

"*Layne.*" Her father sternly warned her with the weight of his voice to mind her place.

"No, I am the one who got the shit end of the stick here. I should get the final say in who gets to handle this on my behalf. This guy comes rolling up here like he's celebrating Halloween, and you're going to trust him to handle this situation?" The problem wasn't that she didn't trust him to handle the job, it was what would happen if he didn't succeed in doing it.

A flash of anger lit up Scott's face that Layne was interfering with things, and it caused a strain in his voice. "You'll have to excuse my daughter; she can get a little opinionated."

The shine of amusement in Joey's eyes was accompanied by a chuckle. "You can say that again."

She was fuming that he found this amusing, and even more so that her father was trying to save face by minimizing her role in the decision-making process.

Meanwhile, Liam was doing his best to stay out of the crossfire. "Let's talk terms. You get a quarter million upfront, and when the job is done you get another half million."

Joey let out a whistle at the numbers Liam pitched to him. "That is a pretty penny, but I have some conditions."

"Name them." Scott leaned forward in his seat, willing to hear what else this was going to cost him.

He nodded over at Layne with a shit-eating grin underneath his mask that no one could see. "Drop her security detail."

No one had expected that caveat, and Liam in particular outright laughed. "You're kidding, right?"

"Do I look like I'm trying to be funny? I've done my research and seen the guys you have posted. I could have dropped each one of them before they had time to shit their pants."

Her eyes settled on her dad's face, trying to gauge what was potentially going through his mind. Not having her security detail would be a godsend in terms of having privacy.

"I can make sure she will be safe, but I can't have your crew getting in my way if I'm going to do the job and do it my way."

"Done. Anything else you want to add?" Hearing that, Liam rose up and saw himself out of the room before he did or said something stupid that he would regret.

"I'm going to need a moment of privacy with her, so I can set some ground rules and expectations."

Scott looked over at Layne. "I will be right outside."

"I will be fine, I can handle Mr. Theatrics over here." She reassured him.

Her father was a little hesitant but was willing to play

ball with this particular man's terms if it meant removing a major player from the field and keeping his family safe.

After the door shut behind her father, Joey rose to his feet, his look enough to leave Layne feeling her body temperature rising. He crooked his finger, motioning her over to him. She obliged, and once she got over to him, she shook her head. "You can't take this job."

"Shut your sexy mouth." He yanked on his belt, pulling it in one slick motion from the loops dropping it to the floor. "I'm calling in that favor you owe me." He made quick work of the button and zipper of his pants as his swollen erection sprang forth.

She looked down at his thick length which was rearing and ready to go. Coyly she looked back up at him. "I don't know, this seems like a conflict of interest."

His hand grabbed her by the back of the neck dragging her in a little closer as he lowered the volume of his voice. "So help me, Layney, you've had me so fuckin' hard all week. If you don't get on your knees like a good girl, I will make sure that you can't walk straight for a month."

Layne tugged down his mask and locked her lips onto his, then pulled back as she lowered herself down in front of him, maintaining sultry eye contact the entire descent. "Get on my knees, just like this?" Oh, she knew she was being a tease and was enjoying every moment. Her hand wrapped around his stiff member, guiding him into her mouth one delicious inch at a time.

One of Joey's hands tightly clamped onto the back of a chair while the other held onto the back of her head. "Ah, yes." He hissed as her mouth slowly slid over him. Layne relished the taste of his flesh, feeling him press deeper into the back of her mouth. Moving her head back, she dragged her tongue along the underside of his cock.

He groaned. "That's it, Layney. Damn, you suck cock like such a good girl." She bobbed her head back and forth on him.

Joey's breaths grew heavier. "I have two simple rules. Rule one, I set the rules and you're going to follow them. Rule two, you don't go anywhere without me knowing." Her hand came up between his legs, gently cradling his sack while her mouth worked its way up and down his size, drawing a whimper from him.

There was a sense of danger and urgency in the air around them knowing that Scott and Liam were both just in the hallway right outside the door.

She eagerly continued to suck on him, his sounds of approval encouraging her even more. His hand began to push against the back of her head to control her movements on him, forcing himself even deeper so that his tip was prodding into the back of her throat.

Joey moaned as the tightness of her mouth sent him spiraling. Each time he felt her gag reflex on the edge of being triggered around the head of his dick, he held himself deeply in her throat for a moment before continuing to thrust.

Gasping for breath, he glanced down at her face, seeing her looking right back up at him while taking all of him in her mouth. He shuddered and shoved himself fully forward. "Fuck, yes!" His hips jerked as his thick ropes of cum erupted out of his dick and straight into her throat.

Layne swallowed it down as her hand ran up over his tensed abs.

After the spasms slowed down and eventually ceased, she withdrew her mouth off him, giving a playful lick to his tip causing it to twitch before she stood back up. Layne smiled proudly at him, seeing how unraveled he was after finally getting his release.

She slowly ran her tongue over her lips, collecting the last tastes of him. "Feel better?"

He pulled himself back into his pants and began closing up shop. "Your mouth is a hell of a weapon."

A knock came to the door before it popped open, Liam partially stepped inside. "Are we done here?"

She looked at Joey with satisfaction in her own emerald eyes at a job well done. "Yeah, I'd say so." Layne stepped around Joey, pausing, and whispering to him, "Good luck with Rule One." She approached the door and left into the hallway.

Liam stood there for a moment eyeing up the masked stranger. "We will drop off the deposit at our previously agreed upon location." His eyes turned cold. "Oh, and don't forget your belt." Then he stepped back outside.

CHAPTER EIGHTEEN

As Layne stood outside the entrance to Death's Door, her father leaned down and gave a quick peck to her cheek. "You let me know if you run into any problems with this guy, ok?"

"I'm sure I can handle it." She gave him a reassuring smile to help him be put at ease.

Scott didn't look entirely convinced, but he was doing his best to give Layne enough space to make more decisions.

Liam stepped outside, immediately drawing a cigarette from the pack tucked in the inside pocket of his suit jacket. While he flicked open a black metal lighter, he stared at Layne with something in his eyes that she didn't quite understand.

"I'll drive you home." He said while the cigarette was wedged between his lips. The flame quickly lit the tip of it as he took a drag.

"I can get myself home just fine." Once again here she was being treated like someone who had no voice.

"Liam will drive you home," Scott interjected, making it a firm decision with the tone of his voice.

She made the effort to not make a mountain out of a molehill by sucking in a breath of cool air. "Fine." It was as polite of a response that she could muster.

Her brother removed the cigarette, holding it between his pointer and middle fingers as he exhaled a stream of smoke. He pointed over at the dark blue sedan parked underneath the sole street light on the block.

Layne got herself into the passenger side, leaning back with a sigh while she waited for Liam to join her. He stood out on the sidewalk speaking with their father another minute or two before parting ways.

When he took his seat behind the wheel, a half-smoked cigarette still in his hand, Layne glanced over at him. "I could have just taken the subway like a normal person. It's right on the corner."

He took one long and final drag from the cancer stick before pitching it out his window. "Just what the hell are you doing?" The white stream of smoke escaped from his mouth as he spoke.

She motioned to what she thought was obvious by making a gesture at the gear shifter. "Waiting for you to drive me home."

His hand smacked the top of the steering wheel. "That's not what I'm talking about!"

She sat there blinking a few times at his sudden outburst, unclear what was triggering him.

He didn't make her ask for more clarification. "With *him*. What the fuck, Layne?! Do you think I'm stupid?" Liam pointed to his temple for emphasis.

Still in a state of shock that Liam was this riled up, she sat there silently trying to even come up with an explanation.

"Li, I don't know wh——"

He turned in his seat to face her. "You just go around sucking any dick that presents itself like a fucking whore?!" His sudden outburst startled even her, having never seen him this bent out of shape before.

"Fuck you! You're one to talk when you chase anything with two legs and a set of fake tits!" Her hand yanked the door handle and swung the door open.

Liam's hand latched onto her upper arm, squeezing painfully hard. "No, you don't get to embarrass our family."

Layne winced as his hand prevented her from getting out of the car. "Ow! Let go, Liam!"

His fingers dug into her even more when she strained to pull away. "Close the damn door, Layne, we're not done here!" An intensity was in his eyes that sent chills down her spine.

When his driver's side door suddenly opened up, his grip loosened up inadvertently. A pair of hands gripped onto his suit lapels and extracted him out of the car.

Layne stepped out of her door to look across the roof of the vehicle to see one livid, masked Joey standing there with Liam in his grasp. Joey's hands harshly shoved her brother back against the side of his car, pinning him there with an unmatched rage in his gaze.

"You put your hands on her again, and I will break them," he growled through gritted teeth. "One bone at a time. Do you understand me?"

Liam was breathing heavily as his rage was going from a rolling boil and coming down to a mild simmer. "Only if the same applies to you."

She shoved herself between the two of them to break up the pissing match. "Enough!" She placed her hands on the front of Joey's chest, looking up at him. "I'm fine. Okay?" Then she half-turned to look at Liam who was brushing himself off and straightening out his clothes, "Go home."

The two boys were still staring at each other with chests puffed out.

"Jesus, just go home, Li." She urged so that the testosterone in the air could at least be brought down by half.

He shook his head, clearly annoyed and he got back into his car. He pulled out of the parking spot, tires squealing as he took off down the street.

Once he was gone, she looked at Joey with a sigh at this mess that was now on their hands. Crossing her arms in front of her as the night air began to bite at her skin she stepped up onto the sidewalk. "I don't think you understand, I don't need you hovering over me, waiting to fight my battles for me."

"I don't think *you* understand," he stepped up to her, "it's now my job to fight your battles."

She dropped her arms down to her sides tiredly. "Don't give me that macho bullshit." Layne turned and began walking past the Death's Door entrance towards the other end of the block where there was a sign for stairs leading down into the subway.

"Where are you going?" He didn't move from where he was standing.

"Home!" She called back to him without so much as looking over her shoulder.

He squeezed his hands into fists. This woman was going to be the death of him. She was driving him crazy with her fiercely stubborn temperament. Joey finally gave in and broke into a light jog after her. "Hey, I will take you home. Will you just stop?" He ran down a few steps ahead of her so he could stop her from going any further down the stairs.

Layne stopped short as he blocked her path. "I don't need you to take me home."

He moved one more step closer to her, his height still towering down over her despite the six-inch difference in where he was standing.

"Don't make me ask twice." His hands cradled both of hers.

"And if I do make you ask twice?" He often said it, but now she was ready to call his bluff.

His eyes shimmered with excitement, snaking an arm around her waist and pulling her up against him. "Try me and find out."

Her hands settled on top of his shoulders as she bit into her lower lip and felt her heart skipping every other beat. Layne tried to ignore the fluttering sensation dipping into her lower stomach, but all her senses tended to fly out the window the second he pulled stunts like this.

Before Layne could test him to find out exactly what he would do, his attention shifted to the quarter-dome mirror posted to the top corner of where they were standing, allowing him to see a few MTA police officers approaching the stairway.

"We have to go." He dropped his hold on one of her hands and led her back up the stairs. Instantly picking up on the change in his demeanor and seeing exactly what he saw, Layne didn't ask questions as she followed him back up to street level.

With his hand firmly holding onto hers, Joey led her around the corner to the next block. He cut down the wide alley between two industrial-looking buildings. About halfway down, she recognized the Challenger she had driven the night they both met.

The proximity sensors unlocked the doors as Joey got within a few feet. Without being told, she got into the passenger seat. Joey got behind the wheel, pulling his mask down around his neck now that they were behind illegally tinted glass.

"Friends of yours?" Layne strapped herself in.

"As much as they are yours."

"I'm not the one walking around in a mask like I'm on my way to a Call of Duty convention."

He grinned as he pulled out of the alley onto the street. "Maybe I will use that the next time I get questioned."

Layne giggled at the absurdity of anyone believing that, although in this city you saw a lot of strange characters that nobody batted an eye at. The Naked Cowboy, need anyone say anything else?

When they arrived back at her house, she pulled her arms out of her jacket, tossing it onto the coat rack near the front door. Joey carried a small black bag inside with him, slinging it over his shoulder.

"What's that?" She nodded over at the bag he was carrying.

"A change of clothes."

She put a hand on her hip. "And just why would you need those?"

"Did you think I was going to tell your dad I was going to keep an eye on you and leave you home by yourself on day one of the job?" He set the bag down on the floor at the bottom of the stairs with a light thud.

"First, no one told you to volunteer for this. Second, you can't possibly watch me every second of the day."

"But trying is half the fun." He gave her a sly wink. "Besides, did you already forget the rules?"

Layne rolled her eyes while walking into the kitchen to take a gander at what she had in her fridge. Beer, condiments, her weekly bag of salad mix that she never actually used and needed to be trashed, and a leftover slice of cherry cheesecake Rebecca had dropped off yesterday.

Opting for the decadent dessert, she pulled out the small plastic container and shut the fridge, only to see Joey standing there leaning back against the counter with his arms crossed in front of his muscular chest and his legs comfortably crossed at the ankles while watching her every move.

There was a calculating look in his eyes. She tried to reach around him to the drawer he was blocking, but he didn't move. "You're blocking my silverware drawer."

"You look a little agitated." A real Sherlock Holmes here picking up on her irritation, wasn't he?

"Agitated? No, I'm frustrated. I'm frustrated because somehow you have managed to work your way into my business. I don't mix my personal life with my business dealings, and yet here you are. I'm frustrated that you have me *frustrated*, when this," she motioned back and forth between the two of them, "should have been a one-time casual encounter."

He had the audacity to smirk at her while he stood there listening to her rant about her frustrations. Joey reached out, took the cheesecake container from her hand, and set it on the counter next to him. Without a word, he snatched her up and flung her over his shoulder with ease.

She found herself very suddenly staring down at his nice-looking cargo-clad ass. "Joey! I'm being serious!" He carried her upstairs to her bedroom, dropping her down onto her bed like a ragdoll. She bounced against the mattress with a squeak. "What are you doing?!"

"Going to take care of your frustration." He pulled the bottom of his shirt up and over his head, exposing the hard physique of his upper body decorated with all of the tattooed artwork.

He didn't need to say it to her twice. Layne quickly disposed of her clothes, wildly flinging them off to the side. Not a second after Joey dropped his pants, he pinned her down underneath him. She buried her fingers in his hair as she pulled herself up to latch her mouth onto his out of raw lust.

His hands ran up her legs, pushing them apart to expose her sex, glistening with her excitement. While his tongue forced its way into her mouth to explore her addictive taste, he lined up the head of his shaft with her opening.

Breaking herself away from his mouth, she showered his face with several more hasty kisses. "Don't you dare make me wait. I need you."

As soon as she said those last three words, he sheathed himself deeply into her. "Fuck, Layney, you have been waiting for my cock, haven't you?"

She cried out as he pushed himself into her in one go, welcoming the sensation of pleasure and the way her body was forced to take him. His hips began pumping his dick into her, losing himself in the moment. His hand slid between them, his thumb circling over her aching clit. The second he made contact, her hips bucked at the intense sensation as she yelled out a series of unintelligible words.

In a few firm strokes of her swollen clit, Layne's body shook to her core with an otherworldly orgasm that had her vision hazy as her pleasure-filled screams filled the air. He continued to grind himself deep into her, groaning out loudly as her pussy locked down around him.

Staying buried deep inside of her, his arm slid around her back and pulled her upright with him as he sat back on his heels, so she was straddling him. His hands ran down her back and possessively grabbed a handful of her firm ass with each hand and began rolling her hips against him.

Layne was still trembling like a leaf from her explosive

release moments ago, her arms wrapped around his neck, keeping their bare bodies in contact. She rode his cock at a slow and steady pace as she recovered from the intensity that had surged through her body. However, she quickly unleashed the hunger that was still gnawing at her for more of him.

"I need more of you." The intimate position had her staring right into his eyes as she panted from the intensity of the sensations her body was experiencing.

"I've got all night planned to take care of my good girl." He nuzzled his face into the side of her neck, trailing hot kisses along her throat as he handled her ass to encourage her to ride him more vigorously.

Joey kept good on his promise and used the rest of the night making sure Layne had her fill of him, until she was left with a mess between her legs, a sheen of sweat slowly drying on her skin, and pure satisfied bliss overcoming every inch of her body.

CHAPTER NINETEEN

The next several days were spent trying to assess what type of normal there was going to be between Layne and Joey. He had two tasks on his plate: keeping her safe while simultaneously plotting out how to fulfill his obligations to the head of the O'Reilly family on repaying Michael Franzetti for his unfortunate decision to try and snuff out Layne's life.

It wasn't going to be a quick process getting a plan of action in order if he was going to do this the right way. Layne had been sending her resources out to gather some information from Franzetti's weakest links to assist Joey in making his plans. He wasn't thrilled about her trying to insert herself into the process, but he was losing that battle with the fiercely determined woman he had chosen to put his life and reputation on the line for.

Joey came downstairs freshly showered, wearing nothing but a pair of jeans belted around his waist. His dirty blonde hair looked darker than normal thanks to it still being damp. He grabbed the cup of coffee Layne had set aside on the center island for him and carefully sipped the dark roast.

Partially seated at the kitchen table, Layne had one knee on the chair and the other foot on the floor while she leaned over the table. She was already dressed and ready to start her day in a pair of lightly distressed blue jeans and a snug long-sleeved shirt with a low-cut neckline. Layne flipped through a few texts and emails on her phone.

Noticing the way her curves fit into those jeans, he smiled. "Coming downstairs to this view every morning is something I could get used to."

"I think you've seen enough of my ass to last a lifetime," she said not even looking up from her phone.

He approached her, pulling her phone from her hands. "And I will continue to appreciate it for at least two more lifetimes."

She finally looked over at him as he confiscated her phone, and whatever she was about to say was replaced with a silent stare at the fine-looking shirtless specimen standing next to her. A smile tugged at the corner of her mouth before she plucked the phone right back out of his hands. "I have work to take care of today, some things have come up."

"We can talk about it after I get something to eat. I'm starving." He patted a hand to his defined abdominal muscles.

She rested a hand on her hip. "There isn't anything to talk about. I have business to take care of."

"Not without me you don't."

She silently said a prayer for more patience with this man. "I thought that when you convinced my dad to drop the security detail on me, I would have more leeway. Instead, you're…"

"Up your ass?" He chuckled.

"For lack of a better phrase, yes. And stop looking so smug about it!" Her hand smacked against the center of his bare chest, where he caught her wrist and tugged her up against him.

He nodded his head down to her ear and whispered. "I will quit looking so smug about it when you tell me that you don't enjoy it." With that, he gave a quick peck to her cheek and released her wrist.

It had been a lost cause convincing Joey that she didn't need his overprotective services while she took care of some routine business matters. The best she got out of him was a promise he would stay out of sight, and she wouldn't even know he was there. Layne found that hard to believe, but it was all she could negotiate for now.

She sat in the closed-off backroom of McGregor's Pub, straddling a backward chair at the wooden table that was unbalanced on one of its four legs. Joey was out front sitting at the bar in the same seat he had chosen the night he met her. He was at least allowing her to conduct her check-in meeting with family associates in private.

Two of her men, or more accurately her dad's

employees who reported to her, were seated across the table. Standing off to the side, there was one tall and leggy redheaded woman examining her cheap manicure.

"Gary, explain to me one more time what's going on with Thursday nights at the Brass Mirror." Layne lifted her glass of golden ale and took a long, therapeutic sip as this meeting wasn't inspiring her that the minions were holding down the fort. Brass Mirror was one of a few of their back-room sites in the O'Reilly underground gambling circuit, only the elite received invitations, and even then, those memberships were reviewed and scrutinized quite frequently.

"Diego wants a bigger cut. He said that things have been getting a bit wild and he's had to hire more personnel to keep things civil." Gary was in his seat, bouncing both of his knees like he was sending erratic Morse code. He was close to Layne's age, and yet he was struggling to keep up with the pace of the job.

"Jesus, Gary, could you pop a pill and stop with the damn jittering?" She let out an exasperated sigh. "Tell Diego, he needs to hire better help to replace who he has. He's not getting a bigger cut just because he's a shitty judge of character."

Gary smoothed his hands over the tops of his knees trying to slow the movements.

Layne looked over to his partner in literal crime. "Update, Darin?"

He dug around in his jacket pocket, pulled out a few folded pieces of paper, and slid them across the table toward her.

Layne reached out and took the documents, unfolding them and reading the contents. Doing her best to control the expression on her face, she immediately finished off the rest of the beer in her glass. "Alright, go ahead and follow up on this, and let me know what you find out." She waved the papers at him before shoving them into her back pocket for safekeeping.

"It may take a while, it's been like casting pearls before swine."

Layne raised both her eyebrows at the idiom, but promptly shook her head. "I don't even want to know what the hell that means. Just find out what you can."

"Are we done here, yet?" The shrill voice of the woman interrupted as she crossed her arms over her stomach, impatiently waiting. God, Layne hated dealing with Kristill, and she hated how she spelled her name even more.

Layne motioned for Gary and Darin to be on their way. "Take a seat."

"I'm fine standing," Kristill replied with boredom hanging in her voice.

"I said fuckin' sit, Kristill." Layne's tone getting kicked up a notch at the attitude she was getting.

"I'm fine." She slowly emphasized each word.

Layne pushed away from her seat, stood up, and walked over to the woman with a really bad box-dye hair job. Going toe-to-toe with her, she lowered her voice, letting the seriousness of her voice edge each syllable. "Take a seat, or I will put you in one."

Her eyes looked Layne up and down, appearing unimpressed and unthreatened. "Oh, whatever, Layne. I don't take orders from you."

If Layne hadn't already been in work mode, perhaps she would have backed down from a mouthy hoe, but Kristill was on their payroll and sure as shit knew better. Her hand snatched Kristill's throat, shoving her back against the wall, harshly pinning her there.

"The hell you don't. Just because you fuck Liam when he's bored doesn't make you indispensable. Now, I have a need for your services and there's a nice little bonus attached to it. So, sit your damn ass in the chair." Layne released the girl's throat and backed off allowing her the space and opportunity to comply.

Kristill rubbed her throat, glaring at Layne with a catty snarl, but finally put herself in a chair.

Layne pulled her phone out and brought up a photo, showing it to her. "Have you seen him before?"

After a look at the face on the screen, Kristill shook her head. "No, I would have remembered a hot piece of ass like that for sure."

"Well, today is your lucky day." Layne grinned mischievously. "I'm going to need you to make him a hell of an enticing proposition. He's out sitting at the bar, do you think you can do that?"

She looked up at Layne with a smile of disbelief. "Shit, I'd do that one for free."

"Good, give it five minutes, and then go out there and work your magic." She put her phone away.

Kristill nodded in agreement and immediately pulled

out a compact mirror and a tube of lipstick to jazz up her look. Layne used the floor access to step down into the storage area underneath McGregor's where all the kegs were stored. At the far end of the cramped storage room was a set of BILCO doors where deliveries could be easily made from the alley.

Unlatching the cold metal doors, she pushed one door up to step out onto the street level of the alley adjacent to the pub. She walked down the alley towards the bordering backstreet that ran behind the rundown Irish pub, figuring she was in the clear. Kristill knew how to keep a man distracted for at least fifteen minutes, maybe five minutes depending on the guy.

She rounded the corner of the building and collided with Joey's solid chest, nearly bouncing right off it. Saving her from falling on her ass, his hands gripped her arms and pulled her back to him with a smirk. "You didn't think that was going to work, did you?"

He pressed her back against the back of the building there in the isolated backstreet. She felt the cool brick against her backside as she looked up at him. "I've heard Kristill has impressive flexibility, you probably should have taken her up on her offer."

His hand came up underneath her chin, gently grasping it. "Afraid I will bend you until you break?"

Just hearing the way he spoke those words, the imagery in her head caused a heat between her legs. "I don't break easily."

"Good." Joey tilted her chin up so he could slowly

adhere his mouth to hers in a drawn-out and surprisingly gentle kiss. It was simultaneously sensual and delicate as it stirred up feelings inside of her that prickled along her skin.

Her lips caressed his, reciprocating the energy between them as it seemed that time itself stood still. Maybe it did.

CHAPTER TWENTY

The sweat was dripping down the back of her neck, rolling between her shoulder blades in a slow tickle against her skin. Layne groaned while trying to catch her breath. "I hate you right now."

Rebecca laughed after setting down her kettlebell on the mat between her feet, her own skin dewy from perspiration after a killer workout. After brushing a rogue strand of sunny blonde hair away from her face she shrugged. "That's fine, but you'll love me when you feel how sore your ass is tomorrow after a solid workout."

Layne lay there on the mat, pushing up into cobra pose to feel the stretch all the way through to her stomach. Drawing in several deep breaths, she worked on completing a few more stretches alongside her bestie.

It had been a hectic few weeks, and she hadn't had the opportunity to catch up with Rebecca the way she typically did. Joey had stuck to his word about trying to give her space, so he wasn't breathing down her neck every second of every day. She often wondered if he really was keeping tabs on her or not given how well he blended into the background.

When it was suggested by Rebecca that they meet up at the gym for a much-needed workout sesh and grab a bite afterward, Layne figured it was as good of a plan as any.

"Still on for margs and tacos? A little protein, a little booze, and we'll call it balanced eating."

Layne laughed. "Is there an option just for tequila?"

"Oh boy," Rebecca chuckled. "I didn't realize that you needed girl time that badly."

After they both hit the showers and got changed, they left the gym and headed down to a small Mexican joint that always had late-night specials for bottomless chips and salsa with two-dollar watered-down margaritas.

After dunking another chip into the salsa bowl, Layne shoved it into her mouth as she waited for Rebecca's reaction.

"I knew it, I knew there was a guy." Clearly, feeling vindicated that her best friend Spidey senses had been spot on. "You have been far less chatty, which usually means you don't want to give anything away."

Washing the saltiness of the chip down with the tang of the margarita, Layne winced that Rebecca could read into things that easily. "Look, all I said was there has been a guy. There are always guys, Rebecca, a girl has needs."

"No, no, no. You have specifically avoided talking about this one, and I want all the details." She leaned forward, ready to take in all the salacious particulars.

Layne took pause trying to gather her words, and before

she got the first word out Rebecca interrupted her. "Oh God, he works for your dad, doesn't he? Is he older? Tattooed?" The barrage of scarily accurate line of questioning was fired off quickly.

She blinked several times at Rebecca's sudden conclusions. "No! I mean, yes, he does but… It's complicated. Yes, he's twelve years older, and yes, he's got some tattoos." Layne eyed her bestie warily while pouring her next round of margarita into her glass from the pitcher sitting on the table. She was left wondering if she was that easy to read, and if so, she was going to need to work on that.

"Oo, nice. It's exactly what I've always pictured for you. Does your dad know? Crap, he would flip his lid." Rebecca pondered all the potential fallouts that would transpire if Scott got wind of anyone working for him fooling around with Layne. It had always been a non-negotiable for as long as Rebecca had been around.

"I don't think so, not unless Liam has gone tattling." Layne grimaced thinking about how Liam would be holding this over her head in the future.

Rebecca raised her eyebrows, looking for more information on that little nugget of information.

A little bit of pink flushed over her cheeks. "He may have overheard some things. Either way, it's not a big deal everything has been very casual"

"Liar." It was an aggressive calling-out, even coming from Rebecca.

"What?"

"You did that thing with your left eyebrow when you

lie. Plain as day." She attempted to mimic the little twitch that had given Layne away.

Layne rolled her eyes. "It's casual, Rebecca, you're reading too much into this. You know how I feel about getting too far into the weeds with guys."

Her bestie rolled her eyes having heard this story before. "Yeah, yeah, yeah, I know. Commitments aren't your thing."

"Exactly." Just when Rebecca was going to try and push the issue, Layne gave her a rare look, pleading her to drop it. Being the good and sensible friend that she was, Rebecca didn't press it any further.

After a change to a lighter subject involving Rebecca's adventures in nannying, they wrapped up the chit-chat after a not-so-subtle hint from the workers in the restaurant that they were closing up for the night.

Right outside the cantina, Layne gave Rebecca a huge hug. "I'm still going to hate you when my ass is sore tomorrow and I can't get up the stairs." She teased before letting Rebecca go from the embrace. "Do you need me to walk you back to your apartment?" The apartment building was only four blocks from there, but Layne was willing to keep her friend company to ensure she made it back safely.

"Nah, I'm fine. I will text you when I get in." She waved off any concern that Layne had.

Layne knew better than to offer up a second time and let Rebecca take off to head home. Being that she was all the way downtown, it was going to be a long trip back to the other end of the city. She hoped maybe she could catch the next 4-5-6 train uptown. The station was only a half block away.

When she got there, she heard the train pulling away as she ran down the stairs of the station, watching the train leave just as she made her way onto the platform.

"Shit." Now she was going to have to wait for whenever the next one decided to show up. She leaned up against one of the pillars in the center of the platform as she waited impatiently by herself—just her and the rats that moved between the tracks. Fifteen minutes passed and there still was no train to be found.

"Screw this." She said out loud to herself, figuring at this point it was easier to hail a cab. Just as she got to the bottom of the steps to leave the platform, a train finally pulled in. Layne changed course and boarded it as soon as the doors opened up.

She took a seat in the empty car, relieved to finally be on her way back home. After indulging in several margaritas and an embarrassing amount of chips, she could use some sleep.

Before the doors shut, a small group of men were laughing amongst themselves as they just barely made it onto the train. The doors shut and the train pulled away from the station beginning the long journey uptown.

One of them locked eyes with her and gave an eerie smile, his hand hitting the chest of his closest buddy lightly. "Looky-look at what we got here. I know you."

His two friends leered at her, and then one spoke up. "You're that chick that got the slip on the masked freak." That wasn't oddly specific at all.

Layne stood up from her seat, holding onto the pole in the middle of the aisle for balance as the train jostled along the tracks. "Wow, I've got a reputation now? I'm impressed."

Three of them and one of her—this was going to be fun. She made sure that her feet were planted firmly in a wider stance given the dynamics of the train movement being a challenging variable.

The guys snickered amongst themselves before the leader of the pack took a few steps closer to her. Layne stood her ground, her eyes locked on his as she evaluated his every movement. When he stopped a few inches from her, she gave him his one warning. "Think carefully about what you do next. I would hate for you to end up limping away with your tail between your legs."

"I also heard that the boss got you all," he ran his tongue along his bottom lip, "wet." Internally, Layne cringed at how gross he just made that sound.

One of her eyebrows perked up, and as one of his hands reached out for her, she grabbed his wrist, pulling him off-balance as her other hand pushed on the back of his shoulder to send him face-first into the pole in the middle of the aisle, causing a fracture of his nasal bone, resulting in a gush of fresh blood pouring from his nostrils. He stumbled onto the floor behind her as his two friends were quick to charge at her.

Her hand latched onto one of the straps hanging from the bar to the left and with her hand on the pole to the right, she kangaroo kicked at the two jackasses while Mr. Broken

Nose was shouting a string of profanities behind her. Tweedle-Dee and Tweedle-Dum stumbled back.

The connecting door to the next car back slid open. Joey stepped in, his eyes lit up with a wrathful vengeance as his fists flexed at his sides. He grabbed one of the two men closest to him, pounding a fist to his face, which caused him to immediately drop to the floor like a sack of bricks.

The second thug charged at him, and Joey stumbled back against the now-closed door. He struggled with the man for a hot minute before gaining the upper hand and propelling him towards the glass case that contained the emergency fire extinguisher. The glass shattered and the man was rendered unconscious with several lacerations to the face.

Momentarily distracted, she witnessed one pissed-off Joey show up to the party, a bloody hand wrapped around and seized her throat. A sharp and pointy blade pressed below the bottom of her ribcage. Before there was any time to react, the train made a sudden turn around a bend in the subway tunnel, causing a massive shift in the movement of the car.

She and the lead thug both stumbled, and it was Layne who took advantage of the well-timed opportunity. Her body snaked away from him; his hand smearing a bloody handprint across her throat.

Joey was on top of him before he re-established his footing. The leader's dominant hand was grabbed and twisted until the bones cracked, resulting in the knife dropping to the ground and sliding under a set of seats.

Protective instincts drove Joey's fist into the guy's face, beating him down repeatedly. The fresh blood splattered in various directions with each impact Joey made. Even when the man lost consciousness, Joey's bloody knuckles continued the vicious assault.

"Joey! *JOEY*!" Layne's hand grabbed his shoulder, forcefully tugging on it to pull him back. The train began to slow as it approached its next stop. "We need to go."

He gave one final strike to the man's face before dropping the body down onto the floor of the subway car. His chest heaving with adrenaline-fueled breaths. The tattoos on his right hand were now covered in the sticky mixture of the man's blood and nasal fluids.

Joey looked at Layne and then the doors as the platform came into view. His bruised hand wrapped around hers, tugging her along with him to the doors that popped open shortly after the train came to a complete stop.

Fortunately, at this time of night, stations outside of tourist areas had very few people. Joey guided her off the train, leaving the three men behind to lick their wounds. After they both got up to street level, he finally paused to turn and face her. His hand softly took her chin, turning her face to inspect for any injuries.

"I'm fine." She fought a wince, feeling the burn along her side now that the adrenaline was fading.

His hand dropped away from her face as he looked over the rest of her, noticing the tear in her shirt. When he went to lift it to take a look, her hands shoved his away. "Let's just get home, it's a scratch."

The fact he hadn't spoken a word since they stepped off

the subway train wasn't reassuring her that he was going to be a happy camper for the remainder of the evening.

Layne would have been nominated the world's biggest liar if she had said that by the time they did make it back to her townhome, she wasn't in a little more pain than she had been willing to admit for a mere scratch on her side.

Once the front door shut behind them, Layne attempted to lighten the mood. "Didn't expect you to run late to the fun back there in the subway."

That was the wrong fucking choice of levity.

Joey glared at her. "I went to take a damn leak, Layne, and just barely boarded the last car before the doors shut."

Getting defensive at his tone, she deflected it right back at him. "And I would have had everything under control until you came and caused a distraction."

"Yeah, you really had things under control." The sarcasm and anger heated his words.

"Don't get pissed at me, I didn't invite the jackasses to come tango." She yanked off her coat, tossing it over the banister. Layne then turned to look at the mirror mounted on the wall, lifting her shirt to reveal a cut where she must have gotten nicked during the scuffle. Examining the wound in her reflection, she tried not to grimace. She wasn't so successful.

Joey took notice and exhaled his frustrations at what had transpired, he was more concerned about making sure Layne was okay. He came up to her, placing a hand on her lower back and motioning at the living room. "Go, sit. That needs to be cleaned up."

Stubbornly she responded. "I can do it."

"It wasn't a suggestion, Layne."

She looked at his eyes in the reflection. Not having it in her to die on this hill, she lowered her shirt and went into the living room. Layne eased herself into one of the armchairs. Joey disappeared briefly, only to return with a first aid kit.

"Shirt off." He commanded.

Layne pulled her arms through the sleeves and eased the fabric up and over her head, dropping the shirt to the floor leaving her sitting there in just her navy lace bra. He pulled up an ottoman and took a seat in front of her as he began sorting the materials he required.

His typically rough hands were surprisingly gentle as he began to clean the three-inch cut on her side. Layne had gotten lucky that it wasn't deep and only needed minimal attention.

"That kick you gave to the two guys though." A bit of pride tugging at the smile settling across his face.

"Impressive, right?" She grinned, only to flinch as he applied pressure to the sorest part of the injury.

"Just about done." He took a few more minutes to fix her up before applying a bandage over it. His hand motioned to the dried blood smeared across her fair skin. "Go get yourself cleaned up. I don't want to keep looking at the reminder that another man's hand was on that pretty little throat of yours."

CHAPTER TWENTY-ONE

Scott O'Reilly stood there peering into the massive fish tank taking up most of one wall of his office. The vivid combination of colors among the various species provided a calming visual. He had several orangey-red Discus, a school of Cardinal tetras, and his favorite: the German Blue Ram. The entire community of fish swam peacefully in the tank.

Behind him stood Joey, hands in his pockets comfortably as he waited for his current employer to explain the purpose behind the meeting he had called. As per his standard protocol, his mask stretched across the bottom half of his face. Also present was Layne, relegated to leaning back against the office door merely for observation. A few feet to her left, Mick stood there with a sour look on his face as he disapprovingly stared the masked contractor down.

Scott finally spoke up. "Beautiful creatures, aren't they? Living their lives to the fullest, blissfully unaware of what exists outside of this ecosystem. At any point, I could play God and drain the water from the tank, leaving them all unable to survive. Yet, they don't fear that. It must be nice."

Unclear where this line of conversation was leading, Joey chose not to interrupt. Scott turned to face him, locking him in his gaze. "I'm not fond of the idea that Layne is as close to this entire Franzetti ordeal as she is. Where are we with resolving everything?"

Layne rolled her eyes at the overprotective sentiment her dad had.

"I don't disclose my methods but rest assured that things are very close. Your daughter is in good hands, and it will stay that way. I have no intention of allowing her to get caught in the crossfire." Joey maintained a professional demeanor in responding to Scott's inquiries on the status of things.

"I'm going to need more assurance than just your word. There's a lot of talk going on in the shadows and tensions are coming to a snapping point. When can I expect you to deliver what has been promised?" The typical O'Reilly impatience that ran in their blood started to present itself.

Joey spoke matter-of-factly. "For everyone's safety, I can't give you that information. You hired me for my methods and discretion, not for a sloppy rush job."

"I didn't expect you to wait until he keels over from old age either." Scott's irritation weighed on his words. He approached his desk, perching on the corner of it. "Let's make sure we don't have a conversation about timeframes again, understood?"

"There will be no need for it, but let me be clear, I will

not be pressured into making a move before the time is right. He will be dealt with. Until then, I'm not going to answer summonses to explain my methods." Not too many men presented a backbone to Scott, but Joey was standing tall.

Scott chuckled with amusement. "You've got some stones, I will give you that."

Finally deciding to interject, Layne spoke up as she pushed away from the door. "It will be done when it's done. I want this wrapped up as much as anybody else. I want to see karma smack Franzetti in the face so hard that he is reduced to a groveling wreck."

Her father gave her a disapproving look, opening his mouth to correct her, but she put her hands up. "I know, I know. You want me to stay out of it."

He pinched the bridge of his nose tiredly. "There are days I wish you were still on the other side of the country, away from all of this." Scott sighed and looked at the two of them. "I want this finalized as soon as possible. I'm not getting a good feel from all the talk around the city."

Joey nodded in agreement that the pulse throughout the criminal underworld was uneasy. "It won't be much longer."

"Good. Now, I have an appointment to get to. Keep me apprised if anything changes." Scott stood up from the corner of his desk.

They all said their goodbyes with Scott wrapping his arms around Layne in a protective bear hug. He pulled back to look down at his daughter. "I meant what I said. It is too big of a risk to have you poking around." He pressed a kiss to the top of her head.

Scott walked both Layne and Joey to the door, opening it up for them. Once they saw their way out, Mick stopped at the doorway looking at Scott. "I don't like this. I don't like him. I wish you would have brought me in on this sooner."

Scott shook his head. "I couldn't."

Not liking the response he was getting, Mick pressed on. "What makes this different than anything else?"

Scott chose each of his words carefully, "I needed to be sure. It's a delicate situation that could drastically change the dynamics of power as we know it." He didn't expound upon what he had needed to be sure of.

"I've never known you to hold back. You aren't going soft now are you, old man?" He gave a playful jab to Scott's arm. Mick looked at his lifelong friend, seeing a man who once had the vicious tenacity of a bull in the ring. Now? He saw this life wearing him down little by little.

Joey pulled away from O'Reilly Manor in his car, with Layne taking up shotgun.

"Why didn't you just tell him?" Layne's eyes were full of curiosity.

"Tell him what?" He kept his eyes straight ahead, focusing on the road.

"That you have a plan." Her hand reached over and rested on top of his thigh.

"Because the fewer people that know the better. The only reason you know as much as you do is because you have this knack for not leaving things alone." As he felt her hand touch him, it caused him to think about other things that she wouldn't leave alone, and he definitely didn't mind it in the least.

"And here I thought you were going to say it was my unparalleled charms."

He cracked a smile, glancing over at her.

Layne put her other hand in her coat pocket, only to find it empty. "Oh, hell." She frowned.

"What?" Joey raised a questioning brow.

"My phone is missing. It must have fallen out of my pocket back at the house. Can you turn around real quick so I can grab it?" She couldn't believe that she hadn't noticed it fall, but it was the only conclusion that was reasonably logical.

Joey already began the process of backtracking. "Are you sure you had it?"

She nodded. "Positive. Liam texted right after we got there saying he couldn't make the meeting today and would just get an update later. He's probably with Kristill." Whatever her brother saw in the paid piece of ass, she would never know.

Minutes later, they were right back at her dad's house. Leaving Joey in the car, Layne hopped out and jogged up the front steps. Once inside, she ran into Mick pulling his arms through the sleeves of his coat by the door.

"Back so soon?" He grinned as he adjusted the collar of the grey coat.

"Hey, yeah. You didn't happen to see my phone lying around here, did you?" Layne was already looking down at the floor to trace back her path.

"You mean this phone?" He pulled the device out of his pocket and held it up for her to see.

Relief flooded her face. "Yes, thank you."

Mick handed it over to her. "Your dad found it on his way out. I was just about to bring it to your place, but you beat me to it."

Layne stood on her tiptoes to wrap her arms around Mick's neck in a quick hug. "You're a lifesaver, I appreciate it." She smiled at him, and he returned the same.

Layne turned to head right back out until she heard Mick speak up. "Layne?"

Her hand still on the door handle she looked back over her shoulder. "Yeah?"

His hand rested on her shoulder in a caring gesture. "I spoke with Liam, and he told me everything. You know how much I care about you, but this guy is the worst type of scum. I haven't said anything to your dad, but you need to quit fooling around. You're going to end up getting burned, and I hate to think what the fallout will be."

Her face fell hearing how much the man she considered an uncle was concerned about her and Joey. Of course, he had heard it from Liam to boot. "I know what I'm doing."

"Do you? Because from what I'm seeing, you are being careless. You have worked so hard to get where you're at, are you so quick to put it at risk? I'm only saying something because I'm concerned." His hand gave her shoulder a squeeze before he continued. "If your dad found out, you and I both know it would be game over. All the progress you've made wouldn't mean anything. It would be back to square one where you were three years ago and there would be no coming back from that."

She shook her head. "I know you're trying to look out for me, but there's nothing to be worried about."

Mick's forehead was all wrinkled up in concern. "Just give it some thought, 'kay?"

She nodded before slipping out the front door. Layne knew he was coming from a place of concern for her, but she wasn't the same girl she was three years ago. She wasn't going to let her father dictate every aspect of her life to shield her from the grit and grime of a life in this business of organized crime.

When she returned to the car, she shut her door roughly, prompting a look from Joey. "Everything okay?"

"Liam is an ass determined to undermine everything I do."

"What else is new?" He put the car back in drive, pulling back into the roadway.

CHAPTER TWENTY-TWO

With Liam being extra ornery, Mick voicing his concerns, and plans being slow to come into place after the not-so-peppy pep talk her dad had with Joey, she was beginning to burn out from all the stressors taking a toll on her life.

Tonight, Joey insisted on taking her to one of her favorite restaurants, a low-key burger spot that had the best bacon cheeseburger she had ever tasted. As much as she argued about going out and wanted to sit and stew at home, he had been right to drag her out. A good meal and change of scenery had helped tremendously. Not to mention the company hadn't been half bad either.

Having Joey around all the time had naturally become an expectation. Things between them were growing more and more complicated in some ways and in other ways? To put it simply, Layne hadn't opened any of her dating apps in weeks.

Leaving the restaurant, they stepped out onto the sidewalk together. The holiday lights had just gone up last week on most of the storefronts indicating the approach of the very merry season. She didn't like to admit it, but the city this time of year was always capable of lifting Layne's mood.

Her fingers slid between his as she held onto his hand for warmth. "I definitely enjoyed that."

A proud smile slid across his face. "Which part? The food or the way I had you squirming in your seat?"

Layne nudged a shoulder up into his side as the heat crept up onto her cheeks and let out a soft laugh. "Both."

With Joey's Challenger currently in the shop until tomorrow for upgrades, they had opted to take one of her two cars. It was parked about a half block down from the gastropub they had just eaten at. She pulled her keys out of her jacket pocket and hit the remote start to get the engine rolling to warm up the interior of the car.

Next, what sounded like a loud crack of thunder filled the air, followed by a rumbling of the ground underneath their feet and a sudden flash of heat. In the vicinity of where her car was parked, an explosion rocked the area with a furious mix of metal, glass, fumes, and flames. Lucky for them, they were far enough from the blast that they were barely outside the edge of potential harm. A few people who had been too close to the blast were not so lucky.

The bomb that went off was strong enough to take her off guard and Layne stumbled into Joey. Protectively he wrapped his arms around her, drawing her closer into his chest and turning in case of any flying debris. Her ears were ringing, dulling the sounds of people screaming and yelling at the violent scene that had just unfolded in front of them.

Once Joey was sure that everything was in the clear, he pulled Layne away from his chest and held her face in his hands as he looked at her. "Layne? Are you hurt?"

The typically unshakeable Layne O'Reilly was visibly trembling. Her eyes were still focused on the remnants of that burning vehicle that used to sit in her garage. Deep inside her brain, her memories rushed back to vividly relive one of the worst days of her life…

A young Layne at barely ten years old shouted back at her mother. "Why can't I go to Rebecca's?! It's not fair! You and dad never let me go hang out with my friends!"

Shannon O'Reilly, with her hands resting on her hips, sighed as she was about to repeat herself for the fortieth time in the last hour.

"I told you Layney, not tonight. Things are very hectic for your dad at work right now. I have already repeated myself multiple times, you can spend the night with Rebecca another day, okay?"

Layne stomped her foot in anger. "Why are you being so mean?!"

Her mother frowned at her slightly, feeling terrible that her daughter was too young to understand. "Layney, it's for your own good. Now, go upstairs and start getting ready for bed."

To continue putting on a display of how displeased she was, she stomped off past her mom to hide away in her frilly pink room upstairs. Once she was slowly calming down from her outburst, she sat in the reading nook set into her bedroom window. Drawing her knees to her chest and resting her chin on top of them, she watched what was going on outside in front of the house.

Her mom stood a few feet out from the front door, leaning in to press a kiss to her dad's mouth briefly. Shannon's hand patted the side of his arm, and she gave him that sweet smile that could warm a million souls. Layne's mom followed the walkway to where her car was parked right out front. When she got inside, she sat there for a minute, and then that's when the explosion happened. Layne bore witness to that great flash of fire blossoming, felt the rattle of the windows of the house, and experienced a sudden onset of fear seizing her heart.

Her mother was in that car. If Layne had gotten her way, she would have been in there with her to be brought over to Rebecca's house. It was the darkest day of Layne's life riddled with grief and guilt, accompanied by a gruesome visual of the personal attack that robbed her of her mom.

Joey shook her by her shoulders. "Layne! Layney, look at me!" Suddenly, she was mentally back there in the present, on the sidewalk with him. She blinked her eyes several times, trying to refocus on what had just transpired. Smelling the distinct burning of various fluids and metal it caused her chest to seize up. She felt like she was beginning to suffocate, and she couldn't get enough air into her lungs which felt constricted, not helped by the shakiness of her body.

"Oh, God, I... I... I... Can't breathe. I can't..." Her

hand went to her chest, searching for any sign that her heart was still beating in there. The more she thought she couldn't breathe, the faster and shorter her breaths were as she heaved in response to the traumatic memories that were physically overcoming her.

"Yes. You can." Joey kissed the top of her forehead, clutching onto her and bringing his face up close in front of hers to force her to come eye-to-eye with him. "Look at me! We have to get out of here. You're fine, I've got you." Holding her close to his side, he was quick to hurriedly walk her away from the burning heap of metal.

Joey's eyes were on the lookout for their surroundings as he escorted her off to some place further away and safer than their current location. After several minutes he sat her down on a bench. He squatted down in front of her, placing his hands on top of her knees as the concern flooded his eyes. "Just try to breathe."

Tears were stinging her eyes as she shook her head with certainty. "I… can't."

His hands began to gently rub up and down over her legs to provide reassurance. "Yes, you can. Focus on me."

Layne's lower lip quivered as she shut her eyes tightly, forcing the tears to trickle down her cheeks. After a few minutes of keeping her eyes closed like that, slowly she was finding a bit of ease in her chest. "It's happening again."

"What's happening again?" He inquired, keeping his words soft.

"My mom… She…" Layne couldn't even bring herself to speak the words as to what transpired over fifteen years ago to her mother. Thankfully, Joey didn't make her say it either.

He stood, wrapping his arms around her as a cloak of protection. "Shh, it's okay. Nothing is going to happen to you, I won't let it."

Layne felt him kiss the top of her head, while the strength of his arms remained locked around her. He continued to hush into her ear. It felt like an eternity that he sat there while he let her work through the emotions that had overtaken her. Gradually her trembling ceased, and she felt calm enough to open her eyes.

Joey hooked a finger under her chin and lifted it to face him. "We will figure this out. Someone wanted to scare you. I will find whoever it is, and I guarantee you, that fucker will regret the day he was born."

Normally, Layne would have argued that she didn't need a man to go off and fight battles on her behalf, but she was too emotionally wrecked to argue with him. She also trusted that he would do just as he promised her: this person would pay dearly.

CHAPTER TWENTY-THREE

Once Layne was settled down enough, Joey took her back to his apartment. She sat down on the cushy sofa, leaning back. Joey brought her over a heavy pour of straight Jameson in a rocks glass. "Drink this, it will help."

He didn't have to tell her twice. She took a small sip at first but then parted her lips more to suck down more of the liquid gold. It didn't take long for the alcohol to take the edge off. Layne offered him up a light smile. "Thank you."

"Thank me when I pull the spine out of the asshole that set off that explosion." His words promised a whole new level of violence to keep her safe.

For a moment she questioned if he actually was capable of going to those lengths, but then she reminded herself of all the things he confessed to her on their first official date together.

Joey continued, "You're not getting more than an arm's length away from me until we get this all sorted."

"What?" Her brain was still struggling to cope with the night's events and even more so as the booze muddled everything so she could avoid an even bigger and epic emotional meltdown.

"You heard me." He leaned over, placing two hands on the back of the sofa on either side of her as he intensely looked at her. "You don't so much as open the door without me. You got that?"

"Don't start with this, Joey. I've got one too many over-protective males in my life as it is." Her hand rubbed her forehead, trying to fend off a headache.

His voice lowered, unwavering in his stance there in front of her. "Then, you have one more to deal with. I'm not fucking around."

She shook her head as she ducked under his arms to get up off the couch. Layne finished the last of the whiskey and set the empty glass on the side table. "The hell I do, I don't need you going all macho man because you think you have something to prove. If I wanted to be controlled, I would have let my dad marry me off years ago."

Joey straightened up, taking his hands off the couch now that she was no longer sitting there. As for Layne, she walked over to the door to his apartment.

"What are you doing?" He asked even though it was obvious.

"What does it look like I'm doing? Leaving. I am not dealing with this bullshit." Her hand slid the chain lock off and twisted the door handle.

Joey's hand shoved the door shut, leaving her unable to jerk it open under his strength. "Did you ever think you're in over your head and actually need to let someone help you, huh? Instead, you're being a stubborn bitch."

That caught Layne's attention, and she turned to look at him, her hands violently shoving his chest, but he didn't budge an inch. "You're one to talk about being stubborn!" She gave him another useless push against the muscles of his broad chest. "Now, stop getting in my way."

"No." His response may have been short, but it carried a heavy weight.

"Argh! See how stubborn you are?!" All of her emotions were bubbling up and now being taken out on him.

Joey wrapped an arm around her waist and hoisted her up, tossing her over his shoulder and walking her away from the door. Layne sharply gasped as she was suddenly flung over his shoulder like his own personal ragdoll to do with as he pleased. Her hands pushed against his back as she squirmed against him.

Dodging her feet kicking up near his face, he carried her into his bedroom and tossed her down onto his bed without any effort to ease the drop. "You're not leaving."

"Oh, fuck you, Joey." Exasperated, she sat up from where she had landed in the center of the mattress.

"Promise?" He tugged his shirt off over his head, dropping it to the floor to be laundered later. His mouth curved into a devilish smile as his bare chest was exposed now, his tattoos that crawled up over his flesh on full display. He knew damn well what effect he had on her when he gave her something to look at.

Layne scoffed but couldn't look away now that he was

standing there half-naked. Damn him. She pressed her hands against the bed behind her. Her own body started to betray her as she felt desire pulsing between her thighs. "I'm not gonna stay here and be watched over like a prisoner."

Joey didn't respond. His hands moved down to the belt around his hips, yanking it open and slowly sliding it out from the loops of his pants. He proceeded to fold the leather belt in thirds, licking his lips as he kept his gaze on her.

Layne's heart began pumping blood a little harder, distracting her from her original intent to leave. Damn her insatiable hormones, they were getting out of control.

"You know what, Layney? You're right." Both of his hands wrapped around the leather belt in front of him.

Was this a trap? Did he really just say she was right?

He approached the bed slowly, continuing, "maybe you're not going to stay here, but you are going to have to make a choice."

"And what choice is that?" Her tongue licked over her lips that suddenly felt dry as her eyes settled on the way he held the belt in his hands.

Joey tossed the belt onto the bed next to her. "Whether or not you can live with walking out that door."

Her eyes softened as she mulled over what he had to say. Joey's hands suddenly took hold of her legs and pulled her so her ass came right to the edge of the bed. He stood there in front of her, the front of his pants eye level with her.

"You either stay and accept that you're mine, and I

always fight for what belongs to me, or you can walk out that door. If you walk out that door, then this," he unbuttoned his pants as he spoke, "is over. Your choice, Layne."

Her eyes looked up at Joey while he stared down at her, waiting for her to make up her mind. Her brain was telling her to walk out that door if she ever wanted to live life the way she had before he interjected himself into it. Every other part of her was screaming to live in the moment and damn the consequences.

"Nothing good can come of this." And she was likely right whether he wanted to admit to it or not. Layne stood up from the edge of his bed, her body brushing up against his. It was a struggle to resist wanting to lay her hands on him, even just for a split second. Catching herself about to do it anyway, she closed her hands into small fists and shook her head.

"We were *never* supposed to get to this point, Joey." All the unspoken apologies were evident in her eyes. Her lips pressed together firmly to avoid spilling out words that would only convince herself to stay.

She walked away from him and made her way towards the exit of the bedroom. Looking back at him would be a huge mistake if she wanted to get further than fifteen steps past the threshold.

Joey kept his eyes on her, keeping a straight face while Layne seemingly made her decision. He didn't make any effort to keep her there.

She placed a hand on the doorframe while pausing her footsteps and did exactly what she told herself not to, she looked back at him.

Cursing under her breath, she couldn't bring herself to walk away from him, no matter what his faults were. Despite the consequences of both of their lives colliding with one another, she tossed it all out the damn window.

She ran back to him, throwing herself at him with her arms wrapping around his neck as she ferally kissed him. There was no hesitation from Joey, he welcomed her mouth as his arms pulled her in against him possessively.

He walked her back until she felt the dresser knobs pressed against her back. Breathlessly she devoured the taste of his mouth. His hands impatiently pulled her shirt up over her head, tossing it off to the side.

"That's my girl." He grinned between feverish kisses as she made her choice to stay. His hands shoved her pants down, taking her panties down with them. "Now, you're gonna show me how much you want to stay."

Her hands unclasped her bra with a single flick of her fingers, letting it slip down her arms and drop to the floor. She smiled as her hands grabbed the waist of his pants, yanking his hips forward closer to her. "In that case, you better be prepared for a long night."

Her full lips were already slightly swollen from the aggressive kisses, and now they were taking a tour of the designs inked over the flesh of his shoulder and down onto his chest. Layne's hands made quick work of his pants while her mouth took things nice and slow.

She lowered herself down in front of him while her lips drifted further south on his body. Her fingers played with the waistline of his underwear, and just as she laid one more kiss on his lower stomach right where the thin line of hair began to lead down into his boxer briefs, she rose back up with a look of hunger in her eyes. Layne playfully pushed him back, until she got Joey onto his back on the bed. She stripped him of the last piece of clothing between the two of them.

Layne crawled onto the bed, sliding her bare body against his. The hardness of his erection pressed against her lower belly.

"You're so fuckin' beautiful, even when you're a pain in my ass." He stared at her in awe that he had her all to himself. Joey's hands tangled themselves into her hair, pulling her up to capture her lips with his. The slickness of the lips between her hips teasingly brushed against his cock, eliciting an excited groan from him.

Pulling back from him just enough to keep their mouths lightly caressing one another as she spoke. "You sure that you're willing to put up with me?"

"Only if you're going to be a good girl for me." The sparkle in his eyes made her all the promises in the world, and she was going to believe in all of them.

Layne smirked as she whispered into his ear. "You mean, like this?" She guided her body down onto his cock, feeling him sink deep into her hot and ready pussy. He moaned, his hands leaving her hair and firmly grabbing her hips.

Sitting up on him with her body capturing exactly what it was craving, she drove her body against him, riding the length of his shaft with slow and purposeful movements. Layne moaned at the sensation of him stroking her from the inside. Joey growled as he allowed her to set the pace. "I want to see how hard you can ride my cock. Show me how much of a good girl you are, Layney."

"Oh, I'm not going to be your good girl tonight." The look in her eyes held a sinful motive. It captured his attention, especially when she paused the rolling of her hips against him.

"In fact," her hands ran up the series of muscles flexing on his stomach, "I'm going to be a very, *very* bad girl." She could feel his hips pressing up into her and the grip of his hands on her hips trying to get back what she had stopped a few seconds ago.

"Mmm, you know what happens when you're not good for me." He looked up at her, his breathing on edge in anticipation of her next move. Of course, Layne smiled knowingly at exactly what she was doing to him.

As she took up her rhythm again, taking him into her repeatedly, she reached down to where they were connected. Her fingers found her clit, stroking it, causing herself to increase the already intense pleasure she was feeling. Her body squeezed around him even tighter as she circled her sensitive bud. Joey's eyes were saturated with desire as he watched Layne touch herself and make those moans of excitement.

Unable to hold back any further, he flipped them over so he was now in control over her. "You still want to be a bad girl?" He gave a hard pound of his throbbing member into her to make sure he captured her attention.

She pushed her hips up against him to feel him as deep in her as she could, a bratty smile dancing across her lips.

"You're just mad that I was in charge, and you actually enjoyed it."

He gave a hard nip to the side of her neck before licking the red mark he left on her skin. "Oh, Layney, you have never been the one in charge."

He wasn't wrong, they both knew it, and it scared the crap out of her that she was losing herself within the chaos they had created for themselves.

CHAPTER TWENTY-FOUR

Things with the car bomb had gotten far too close for comfort for both Layne and Joey. While it had been a run-of-the-mill scare tactic last night, it was doubtful that the next time they would be so lucky.

Hearing rummaging, Layne rolled over in bed, all tangled up in the sheets. She saw Joey leaning over a large trunk on the other side of the bedroom. He was wearing nothing but a pair of grey boxer briefs that clung over his firm ass providing quite a sight to wake up to. The muscles in his back flexed as he moved objects around inside the trunk.

"What are you doing?" Still trying to shake off the slumber from her voice.

He straightened up and looked over at her, immediately smiling. "I didn't expect you to be up for another couple of hours after last night." Joey came to the bed, crawling across it to greet her with a kiss that felt criminal for this early in the morning.

Her hand ran over the thick stubble on his face as she matched the intensity of his lips working over hers. The fresh scent of soap was clear on his skin indicating he had already taken a shower while she had been catching up on beauty rest. Last night's activities had left her requiring a little extra time to recover. The soreness was already setting in reminding her of each deliciously intense moment they had shared.

When they both came back for air, she sank back into bed with a satisfied smile and a sparkle in her eyes. "You still haven't told me what you were doing."

"Checking my stock in case I need to do some shopping." He got off the bed and retrieved a tee and jeans from his dresser drawer. Layne was mildly disappointed as he pulled the shirt down over his upper body, covering up many of the tattoos she enjoyed memorizing line by line. His jeans and boots were quick to follow as he expanded on his initial response. "I'm going to have to take care of a few things later on tonight."

She frowned. "What do you mean take care of a few things?" Layne had grown adept at reading people, and Joey was no exception.

"Don't worry about it." He pulled his jacket off the hook on the back of the closet door.

Immediately, she tossed the sheets off herself and got out of bed. "Try again." She pulled on some clothes that she tracked down off the floor. Arguing with him while she was naked was about as effective as baking a cake in the bathtub.

He slid his arms into his jacket, still avoiding her question. "I have to go run a few errands, that's it."

She walked right up to him, her finger firmly poked him in the chest. "No, you're not telling me something."

He placed his hands on her arms, kissing her on her forehead to placate her. "I can't sit back anymore and risk that Franzetti is going to slither through the cracks like the snake he is. You and I both know that this entire shitshow needs to come to an end."

"And you were just going to leave me out of the loop, is that it?" She didn't even bother hiding the irritation behind her words.

"That's always been the plan, Layne. Your dad doesn't want you involved, and I don't want you involved. End of story."

He was being so calm about this, and it was only making Layne more irritable. "So, a bunch of alpha-minded men are trying to tell me what I can or can't do?"

He sighed seeing this go down an unproductive path. "You know that's not the case. Look, I know you can stand on your own two feet - I have never doubted that. Shit, I've been on the receiving end of your right hook. This has to be different though. I can't risk you being a distraction or liability and I sure as hell won't put you through the pain and suffering if things go poorly."

"You mean, if you fail and Franzetti sends you six feet under?" Her heart ached even imagining the dark hole of emotions she would go through if that were to happen.

If he was worried about that possibility, he didn't show it. "It's always a risk in what I do."

Her hands held onto his forearms, feeling the muscles flex underneath his skin. "I'm a big girl, why don't you just let me worry about my own sensibilities, hm?"

He moved his hands up to cup her face as he locked his sight on her nearly staring straight into her soul. "No." Then, he released her and grabbed his keys off the top of his dresser. "But if you want to come with me to get coffee and a bagel I won't stop you."

He didn't want to let her out of his sight, but now the tables were turning, and she wasn't going to let him out of hers. So, breakfast and caffeine it was.

It wasn't a difficult choice though, as there was just something about a freshly made bagel piled with an over-easy egg, grease-soaked bacon, and cheese that could lift Layne's mood. Joey took her to a mom-and-pop bagel shop for that delicious breakfast and a strong cup of coffee. But she never let his words leave the back of her mind.

***

Knowing damn well he had some dark intentions looming on the horizon, she had intentionally glued herself to his side all day long.

His arm was wrapped around her there on her sofa while she snuggled up against his side with the television on watching the New York Rangers get their asses handed to them by the Philadelphia Flyers. Things were looking ugly being down 3-0 before the end of the first period.

Joey's phone buzzed, and he took one glance at the message before lifting his arm off her. "I have to go make a phone call." He got up off the couch and began to dial a number on his phone as he left the room.

Layne sat there a few minutes before she straightened up in her seat, straining to hear his voice but she heard nothing at all, not even the pacing of his footsteps.

"Joey?" She got up off the couch and looked into the hallway, finding it empty. Layne walked to her front door, looking out the window only to see his car no longer parked in his typical spot in front of her house.

"Shit!" She ran back into the living room, rushing to jam her feet into the shoes she had left in front of the couch. Layne was hellbent on not being left behind just because everyone thought she needed an excessive level of protection.

When she went to her purse she dug around for the keys to her now only remaining vehicle, each second she didn't find them in the small bag, the more she panicked. Quickly, she realized that he had taken her damn car keys. "For fucks sake!" She hustled into the kitchen to grab her spare set.

Layne grabbed a few more necessities, unsure of what was going to await them and she wanted to be prepared. Once she sat in the driver's seat of her silver Beamer, she ran down the mental list of possibilities of where he was going.

"Think, Layne, think." She had zero care about the aesthetics of holding a conversation with herself out loud as she began narrowing down the most likely locations he would be at. Mentally preparing a preliminary list of spots, she pulled out of her garage speeding down the street.

She attempted several calls to him without any answer. Layne analyzed everything they had ever discussed about the way he ran his operations, Franzetti's patterns, and any minor detail about his vague commentary on how he was going to make his move when the time came. Joey had been careful with the details he shared with her, but not careful enough that she didn't have some guesses on his next moves.

The only question was if she was going to track him down before he took away her chance to serve up her sweet revenge.

CHAPTER TWENTY-FIVE

Things were coming full circle, and Joey decided it would be perfect justice that Franzetti would meet his end down at the very docks where Layne was supposed to meet her fate at Joey's hands. The shoddy building where he had briefly held her captive all those months ago was still situated across the gravel lot.

Thanks to some friendly flies on a wall, he had been able to intercept Franzetti during a small window of opportunity as he was leaving his mistress's home.

Masked up, Joey loomed over Franzetti while a dark and sinister shadow reflected in his eyes. Michael arrogantly held his head up high while he was forced down onto his knees there on the wooden boards at the end of the very same dock Layne should have been pitched off if Joey had done what Franzetti had hired him to do. It was nothing but them and the sound of the water lightly slapping against the supportive pilings of the dock.

"Your time's up, Mike." Joey's head was already in the

grim mind space where he was able to calmly focus on the process of taking someone's life.

The sound of a car door slamming shut in the distance and a small pair of feet pounding against the gravel neared them both. The hell if Layne was going to allow Joey to do this without her there. She had every right to witness the end of this particular chapter of her life. It was going to be her own personal version of therapy.

After trying a few other locations, she had concluded this was the next logical spot to check. Fortune was shining upon her as it seemed she arrived in the nick of time.

Not removing his eyes from the man kneeling before him, Joey sternly spoke to her, "I told you I didn't want you here."

"And I told you...I wasn't going to listen." Her chest rose and fell from the quick sprint across the large lot from where her car was parked.

She took in the sight of Franzetti kneeling there, hands secured behind his back. It appeared Joey had already repaid a few debts to him from the fresh swelling around his eyes and the busted lip.

Franzetti laughed as he saw the two of them standing before him. "What a joke - the two of you. The stone-cold killer turned weak by an uptown bitch who doesn't know her place. Have you even told her? Does she know about your deepest, darkest secret?"

Layne's brows furrowed as confusion settled in as to what type of deep dark secret Michael was referring to. Joey had confessed to his lifetime of crime, and not once had she ever judged him for that. In return, Joey had never judged her for her own lifetime of sins.

A delighted grin popped across Franzetti's face. "She doesn't know, does she?"

Joey's hand grasped a handful of Michael's greasy dark hair, shoving the barrel of the pistol against Franzetti's temple. "Shut the fuck up, you sorry excuse for a human being!" His words seethed with anger.

Layne's fingers wrapped around Joey's arm to give him pause. "Wait! Stop!" She glared down at the man who had brought so much pain and mayhem into her life. If anyone was going to have the chance to eliminate him, she wanted to be the one to do it if she was ever going to sleep at night.

"Don't listen to him, Layne, he's trying to buy time I'm not going to give him." Joey cautioned her, but she ignored his warning.

Her hand remained on his arm which was flexed tight with tension. She wanted to try and make sure that Joey didn't pull the trigger. "No, I want him to think that whatever he says is going to make a difference."

Not even flinching, Franzetti continued to casually speak like his life wasn't about to end within minutes. "I've known Joseph here for a long while. The first job he ever did for me was a doozy. When was it? About fifteen years ago?"

Michael kept his eyes on Layne's face, ready to soak in her reaction as he continued to share the bombshell. "I couldn't risk one of my own men placing the explosive on your mother's car. I needed someone without any known ties to me. I needed someone just like Joseph here. He did such a good job, too. Don't you think?"

The world began spinning around her as she tried to reconcile what Franzetti said. Her hand fell from Joey's arm as she backed up a few steps, staring at the man who had promised her everything. The very same man she had been willing to risk her life, job, reputation, and heart for.

"Layne…" Joey's words to even begin explaining himself were lost. He glanced over at her, regret flooding his face.

Her chest grew heavy while her chin quivered as the vivid imagery of her mother's last moments flashed through her mind. Layne's green eyes—her mother's eyes —began to blur with a well of tears. The tears were packed full of anger, betrayal, pain, and sadness. Her heart was being squeezed by a vise until it released into an eruption of rage.

Her hand pulled her firearm from its holster underneath her jacket and without a second thought, she fired a chain of rounds.

Bang, bang, bang, bang, bang, bang. Click. Click. Click.

The entire contents of the clip were emptied, and even then, her finger still squeezed the trigger several more times.

All the bullets formed a cluster in the center of Franzetti's chest. His body jolted and jerked with each impact until lifelessness overcame him and his corpse slumped onto the boards. The scent of gunpowder, singed flesh, and blood tainted the night air.

There was a moment where Joey thought that she might have shot him as well, and he would have deserved it. He moved slowly, sliding his pistol into his thigh holster, not wanting to make any sudden movements that might startle Layne.

His hand pulled down the front of his mask, exposing his face to her. He placed one boot in front of the other towards her, keeping his palms open and in front of him. The last thing he wanted to do was come off as anything other than harmless.

Her arm was still extended out towards Franzetti's body with her baby Glock still tightly grasped in her hand, but steady it was not. Her entire body shivered from the adrenaline wracking through each of her muscles. Now, tears were freely flowing from her eyes, and when she finally noticed Joey making a slow approach.

"Why?!" Her voice screamed out with all the pain of unanswered questions. Her dominant arm lowered under the weight of the hunk of metal. "WHY?!" She repeated herself, simultaneously hurling the Glock right past him into the water of the depths of the Hudson behind him.

He flinched as the weapon was cast in his direction and barely wooshed past his head. "Layne, please, let's just talk about this." His words were calm and slow as he attempted to de-escalate the situation. Another step forward was taken.

"I don't want to talk about this! I want to know why!" She ran her fingers through her hair, as the tears burned her cheeks leaving a trail of red behind them. Layne closed the last few feet of distance. Her hands harshly shoved him back. "Were you ever going to tell me? Huh?!"

Joey let her create some space when she shoved him, but he didn't let it stay that way. "Was I going to tell you? No, because I knew you'd go fully unhinged before I could explain shit."

She half laughed through the tears in her voice. "Unhinged? That's putting it nicely. She was my *mother*! She was the one beacon of light and love in my life, and you robbed me of her!"

Layne lunged at him. Her fists swung wildly without any mental clarity to support a thoughtful or well-executed attack. The only thing that fueled her right now was erratic emotions.

Easily avoiding any blows, Joey grabbed her wrists stabilizing them. Layne dug her feet into the ground but unsuccessfully planted herself there. Her arms yanked back from his grasp but found herself unable to overcome his strength.

"Layney, I'm so sorry. If I could go back and change things, I would. If I could have seen you coming into my life, then I wouldn't hesitate to fix things. I can solve a lot of things, but going back in time isn't on the table here."

"Fuck your apology!" She flung her weight down to try and free herself from his restraint. He lowered himself down with her until they were both sitting on the ground. He tugged her into his chest and wrapped his arms around her in hopes that he could chase away the agony she was experiencing.

Squirming against him, she let out a scream against his

chest that broke down into heavy sobs. Joey's chin rested on top of her head, his hands soothingly rubbing up and down her spine as she let out all her pain. It wasn't only the pain of knowing his past had violently collided with hers, but it was the pain that couldn't be healed even after taking Franzetti's life for his wrongdoings.

When the tears had slowed, and her sobs had quieted, Joey pulled her away from him slightly and looked down into the bloodshot eyes. "We can't stay here much longer. I need to clean things up. Go wait for me in my car, and I will take you home. I don't want you driving like this. Okay?"

All the emotions left her feeling drained and numb. Layne's face was blotchy from all the tears that had been shed, and her eyes were swollen from crying herself dry. She wanted to argue with him, but she didn't have it left in her, so she simply nodded.

While she went and sat in the passenger seat of the Challenger, Joey took care of the gory task of dumping the heaping corpse off into the churning waters of the river. Shell casings were collected. All evidence of what had transpired was erased.

Meanwhile, Layne sat there studying the mundane-looking dashboard as she tried not to think about the painful truths she had learned tonight. Insult to injury, Franzetti's death didn't even soothe her soul as she had hoped it would.

The driver's side door opened, and she looked over at Joey as he slid into the leather seat. "We should be good to go."

"Thanks." Her voice was quieter than a mouse.

The engine churned to life, and they left the dock behind them. During the ride home, the silence was beyond uncomfortable, yet she didn't care. What was she supposed to say to him? Layne looked out her window, taking in the scenery of passing by various buildings, parked cars, and pedestrians still walking about on the sidewalks and living their dull little lives.

The silence allowed her to begin rebuilding the wall inside of her that Joey had started disassembling from the first moment he had laid his eyes on her. He had effectively begun making a path inside of her heart to allow her to open up. Layne realized that it was her mistake in allowing him to do that.

CHAPTER TWENTY-SIX

Though not his typical parking spot, Joey pulled into the parking garage underneath his apartment building and found a space not far from the elevator.

After the engine quieted, he immediately got out of the car and opened her door for her. "Let's get you inside."

Finally paying attention to their location instead of escaping inside her head, she found herself not where she had expected to be. "You said you were taking me home."

"I will, but I'm not driving all the way uptown tonight. Besides, you look like you're ready to keel over." Was part of his reasoning selfish? Perhaps, but he still felt compelled to ensure her safety even if she currently wanted nothing to do with him.

He escorted her inside, and when she was in the comfort of his unit, she drew in a cleansing breath, trying to feel more at ease. Her body wanted nothing more than to render into relaxation mode, or perhaps a coma.

Joey stood by the front door, hands tucked into his pockets. "A bath will help."

She ignored his advice. "I'm just going to get some sleep on the couch." Her words were heavy with fatigue.

He shook his head. "Not happening. I'm not leaving you to your own devices."

"I'm not in a mood to argue, Joey. Just go into your damn room and leave me alone." She rubbed her hands over her face trying to push away the exhaustion and combined frustration. Yet, he remained right where he was standing without any indication that he was willing to budge.

She looked up at the heavens, at her wits end that he was being his typical stubborn self.

Giving up this particular battle after deciding it wasn't worthwhile, she tiredly looked at him. "Then, make yourself useful and get a bottle of booze." She left to see her way to his master bath, where she began drawing the steamy water for a soak.

Morbidly, she gave a quiet chuckle to herself. Here she was about to take a bath in the same tub that Michael Franzetti had tried to drown her in on the very night she blew him away down at the docks.

While the tub filled, she tossed in a selection of scented salts and aromatherapy bubbles she had stocked Joey's bathroom with over the past couple of months.

Her clothes fell to the cold tile floor piece after piece. Gradually, Layne lowered herself into the heat of the bathwater until she was submerged up to her shoulders.

Leaning her head back against the edge of the tub, she

closed her eyes and tried to clear her mind of everything except the sensation of her muscles relaxing in response to the warmth surrounding her.

Joey appeared in the doorway, a bottle of Sagamore Rye in one hand and two glasses in the other. She cracked open one eye when she felt his presence and peeped over at him before closing her eye again. "I don't need a glass."

He used his foot to nudge a bamboo stool over to the edge of the tub and took a seat on it. Cracking open the bottle, he filled the two glasses. One was handed over to her.

She opened both eyes, and her soapy hand took the glass. "How long are you going to stay in here?"

"As long as it takes." Sincerity and honesty wrapped around his response.

"For what?" Her eyes got lost in looking at the amber liquid sitting still in the glass.

Joey hadn't touched his beverage yet, focusing all of his attention on her. "To know you will be okay."

Layne scoffed lightly. "You might be waiting a hell of a long time."

A small smile tugged at the corners of his mouth. "I know, but you're worth it."

She gulped the stiff liquid to try and squash down how those words made her feel. Fortunately, he didn't press her for small talk while she took some downtime for herself.

With the heat surrounding her in the tub, and the warmth of the rye inside of her, she finally felt a state of nothingness overcoming her. Her brain wasn't yapping in her ear, and her heart wasn't trying to fill her soul with sunshine and rainbows.

As for Joey, he just sat there on the stool next to her while indulging in the occasional sip from his drink.

When her beverage was gone, she handed him the empty glass. "Could you hand me that towel over there?"

Setting her glass on the counter next to the sink, Joey fetched the towel and handed it to her. Without asking, he gave her privacy and exited into the bedroom.

After drying herself off, she brushed her hair out, looking at herself in the mirror as she did so. She could still see the evidence of her emotional outburst all over her face, especially in her eyes. Layne wrapped the towel around her body, securing it in place before she came into his adjoining bedroom.

Joey wasn't anywhere to be seen, but on the bed laid out for her were a pair of royal blue silk pajama shorts and the matching camisole she kept here for overnight stays.

A few minutes later, she emerged from the bedroom in her pajamas to see Joey standing there in the hallway, leaning back against a wall as he scrolled through some messages on his phone. "Where are you planning on spending the night?"

He looked up to see her appear in the hallway, smiling as he admired how stunning she looked even after a hell of a night for both of them. "Where do you want me to?" There were no expectations set in his voice.

She was silent, unsure of what she wanted from him. Seeing her uncertainty, he approached and set his hands on the soft bare skin of her shoulders.

"Go get into bed." He nudged her back towards his room, encouraging her to do as he said. Layne trudged back to the bedroom, glancing back over her shoulder to see if he was following her.

Joey indeed followed, watching as she climbed into bed laying down in the middle with the sheet pulled up to her waist. He stopped at the edge of the mattress, tugged a blanket up over the sheet, and tucked it in around her.

Then, he joined her. Laying on top of the blanket, on his side facing her, he brushed a few rogue strands of her hair away from her face. "Try to get some sleep. I will be right here in the morning."

She looked up at him with eyes full of all her vulnerabilities. "I'm sorry."

Her apology took him by surprise. "For what?"

"That I lost my shit tonight." Layne frowned, hating that she let her emotions get the best of her. She was used to being more level-headed than that. Maybe Mick was right. Maybe Joey was responsible for clouding her thoughts and judgment.

He shook his head, a hand cupping the side of her face. "Shh, you don't have to apologize for being you, Layne. Never apologize for that. I signed up for this, and that includes you flying off the handle. It includes you being stubborn as fuck. But it also includes all the benefits of seeing the way you look at me when you think I won't notice, the way your nose has a cute little wrinkle when you laugh, and the way your voice sounds when you say my name."

Layne's lower lip quivered slightly as his words sank

right down into her heart, past the partially crumbled emotional wall she had tried to reconstruct inside of her.

"Come here." He pulled her into him as he rolled onto his back, leaving an arm around her.

She curled up into his embrace, resting her head on his chest where she could listen to the sound of his heart steadily beating. Layne's eyes fluttered closed and allowed the rhythm of his breathing and the warmth of his body to lull her into a much needed deep slumber.

Unsure of how many hours of sleep she had gotten, she lay there in Joey's bed, staring up at the ceiling cast in the amber light from the street lamp right outside.

The sounds of car horns, emergency vehicles, and hollering from folks leaving the bar could all be heard despite the window being shut. It truly was the city that never slept, and tonight Layne wasn't getting much more sleep.

Her brain wouldn't shut off. It was processing all the scenarios of how all of this could go wrong, all the things she would need to address, who was going to cause problems, and an entire slew of other hypotheticals. Sure, some of these thoughts were warranted, but there was a large chunk that was turned into mountains from molehills - if the molehills even existed in the first place.

The top sheet was still draped over the top of her body, providing just enough comfort from the light air movement from the ceiling fan above the bed. She looked over at the clock on the night table next to her, nearly four in the morning. Joey was lying next to her on his back, his body sprawled out comfortably with an arm tucked underneath his pillow.

He must have gotten undressed after she had initially fallen asleep, as he was now in nothing but his boxer briefs. The sheet was just barely covering his hips. Staring at him, he looked so at ease while he slept.

Admiring his body, it brought her a fleeting moment of reprieve from her harrowing thoughts, but only for them to come barreling back into her mind with a vengeance when she thought about all the challenges he would also face for everything that had transpired to this point. Reality is such a bitch.

She may have pulled the trigger on Franzetti, but Joey would be guilty by association if the rest of the Franzetti clan found out. He had cleaned up her mess. Then, there was the concern that her father would lose his shit if he found out that Joey had been screwing his little girl when he should have been focused on the job.

The real kicker was if it ever came out that Joey had been responsible for installing the explosive device that took the life of her mother. It didn't matter if Franzetti had ordered the hit, it was Joey who executed it. It seemed that she was setting herself up for a life full of pain if she let this continue.

Cringing at the worst-case scenarios, she finally lifted the sheet off her body, moving slowly to not wake him. Layne felt certain she couldn't do this. She would get hurt. He would get hurt. It was all inevitable.

There was no way she could face her deepest feelings, and she couldn't risk things going to hell in a handbasket. She sure as fuck couldn't handle her feelings getting shattered if things did go poorly.

Gathering her clothes that were neatly folded on a chair near the window, Layne stealthily changed from her pajamas into what she had worn that night.

Once she was in Joey's living room, she found a scratchpad and pen. Tearing off a piece of paper, she quickly wrote a message on it. Her eyes stung with unshed tears as she imagined how badly he would take this.

THANKS FOR BEING MY BEST FLING YET. LET'S MAKE A CLEAN BREAK WHILE WE CAN. ~ LAYNE

The tip of the pen hovered over the paper after signing the 'e' in her name, catching herself before she added a 'y' to the end. Abandoning the pen on the paper, she decided the note said all it needed to. Short and sweet.

Layne reminded herself that he wasn't the knight in shining armor, he had said so himself. It still didn't take the ache away from writing off their time together as a meaningless affair.

Leaving his apartment there on the seventh floor of the building felt like trying to pull away from gravity itself. She wiped her fingers underneath her eyes to catch any tears before they fell. Too many tears had already been shed. She scolded herself for being such a little bitch about all of this.

Suck it up, buttercup. There were plenty of other men

out there that weren't nearly as much trouble as he was. A polo-wearing country club type from the Hamptons would be more acceptable, she tried to convince herself. Her leaving things where they were was easier on everybody and quieted the overwhelming thoughts and feelings deep inside of her.

She stepped into the elevator, allowing the doors to seal her decision to end this thing that Joey and her had going on between them.

CHAPTER TWENTY-SEVEN

The next week had been the most difficult for Layne. After the first twenty missed calls and nearly a hundred text messages, she outright blocked his number without so much as giving him any responses.

She should have expected that he would be so persistent despite her note to him, but she naively hoped otherwise for her own sanity. He had gone so far as to show up at her house several times from what she could tell from her security cameras, but she had been spending her time anywhere else except her own residence. Primarily, Layne had been at O'Reilly Manor pretending to sink her free time into work and also where it would be a death mission if Joey tried to show up here.

As far as her father was concerned, the job he had hired Joey for was complete and no one had seen Franzetti. People disappearing unexpectedly in this line of business typically only meant one grim conclusion. Scott wired the balance owed to Joey to the previously communicated offshore account.

The second week after breaking things off, things began to calm down, and by a month later she was considering trying to resume a normal existence again.

Sitting in the cozy reading nook by the third-floor window inside of her old bedroom, she heard her phone ding. When she took a look at the screen, it was a text from Rebecca.

Her best friend was the only person she had confided in, and even then, she only gave the bare-bones version of what happened. Layne had framed it as she determined Joey was bad news with a horrific past and she ended up cutting things off.

REBECCA

Where have you been?

FYI, being a recluse isn't healthy.

LAYNE

It's called soul-searching thank you very much.

REBECCA

Bullshit.

LAYNE

That's your opinion.

REBECCA

That's my statement of fact.

Let's go out tonight. Girl's night only. Eat too much food, drink too much, and dance our asses off somewhere. It would be good for the soul.

Layne cracked an ever so slight smile at the memory of their last girl's night out that had involved hitting up a club. They indeed ate too much, drank too much, and had an embarrassingly good time.

She hated to admit it, but Rebecca likely had a point here. Girl's nights weren't about going out on a hunt for men, but as Rebecca put it: it was good for the soul.

LAYNE

I hate you.

REBECCA

I know. I will meet you at six tonight by the Broadway-Lafayette Station.

Calling it a done deal, Layne sighed out loud knowing that it was time to shake it all off.

That night she met Rebecca right on the corner of Crosby and Houston Streets outside of the subway station. The first order of business was Rebecca dragging Layne to her latest restaurant find. The menu had been all Asian inspired with a twist in the cooking method.

Layne had been hesitant at first, but once again Rebecca didn't lead her astray and the food had been phenomenal. She wasn't much of a foodie, but in New York, there were so many restaurants competing for business it created a demand for each establishment to up its A-game.

During dinner, the two caught up on life. Layne fielded the hard and heavy questions about this tumultuous relationship with Joey. As for Rebecca, she had recently gotten news that the family she nannied for was adding to their clan which meant a pay bump.

After dinner, it was a few blocks down to some club Layne hadn't ever visited before. It was unassuming on the outside, in fact, she probably would have walked right by if Rebecca hadn't said something.

Once they were inside, they were led down a dark hallway and a small flight of stairs before the hall opened up to a large open space, reminiscent of an industrial factory. The music was upbeat with the bass booming loud enough to feel it in your bones.

It was packed with people all looking to either grab drinks at the overcrowded bar or move their bodies in the centralized dance space. Along the perimeter of the room were private booths designated for VIPs with table service. If Layne had known ahead of time, she would have snagged a table for them. It's not like she didn't have money to burn.

As if reading her thoughts, Rebecca leaned in to shout over the thumping of the music. "We don't need a table! We are going to dance all night and have a damn good time!"

Rebecca grabbed Layne's hand and began weaving through the sea of folks towards the bar barely visible by all the people surrounding it. Thankfully, Layne's red heels were sturdy enough to handle the sudden changes in direction wherever an opening appeared between other patrons to squeeze through.

Leave it to her bestie when they got to the bar to bat her eyelashes and lean forward to flaunt the eye candy on her chest as a means of capturing the male bartender's attention. A few minutes later they both had a freshly made cocktail. After taking a sip, Layne knew there were at least two varieties of booze in it, but which ones were difficult to decipher from the mixer masking the taste of the alcohol making it easy going down.

After the first drink worked its magic, Layne was starting to feel more relaxed and starting to realize how much she needed this night out.

"You were right!" Layne shouted over the club-mixed pop tunes playing.

"Of course, I was!" Rebecca gave a massive smile as she continued moving her body to the beat of the music.

With all the people packed in the club putting off a metric ton of body heat, Layne was suddenly glad she had opted for a simple black dress with spaghetti straps. It hugged each curve of her fit figure, over the swell of her ass, and stopped shortly thereafter.

Her hair was down and free to fall over her shoulders and midway down her back. In one hand, Layne held yet another cocktail, she had lost count by now how many she had indulged in. She didn't come here to think about anything, including keeping count of beverages.

It didn't take long before they were both joined by the occasional guy looking to get in on a dance with them. Rebecca with her warm blonde hair and baby blues easily roped in attention. It wasn't to say that Layne didn't attract her own male fans, but she was used to keeping up a front that made her less approachable.

A younger guy came up to her, taking Layne's flash of a sweet smile as an invitation. He looked barely out of college, hardly five-eight, slim but not muscular, and had the whole clean-cut baby face thing going on. He wasn't her type, but that wasn't the point of going out tonight, now was it? She was here to forget all about her go-to type of man.

His hands settled on her hips as she moved them to the rhythm of the song that was currently on full blast. Gradually, the minimal space they had was fully eliminated when some drunk girl knocked into Layne, causing her to stumble forward right up against the guy's chest. "Oof!"

The buzz of the cocktails was kicking in full-time by this point, and she couldn't help but give off a giddy smile as she looked up into this guy's dull hazel eyes.

Once the song started to transition to the next, she looked around the guy's shoulder to see if she could lay eyes on Rebecca.

Not seeing her bestie, she leaned in a little closer to the guy so he could hear her. "I will be right back!" She patted his arm reassuringly before stepping away to navigate through the mobbed dance floor.

Layne considered texting her phone, but it was unlikely the shitty reception would allow it in here. What was likely was Rebecca was waiting in an insanely long line for the women's restroom, but she needed to make sure her friend was okay since she had gone off without saying anything. The only problem was she had no damn clue where the bathroom was in this place.

Layne finally shook her head. "Fuck this," and squeezed past a few more folks until she let herself into the VIP table area which was raised on a platform on the perimeter of the space. Her hands grabbed the railing designed to prevent the drunks from falling off the platform, and she leaned against it, straining to see across the crowd to see if she could spot the bathroom from here.

Some random girl at the table behind her stood up and tapped the back of Layne's shoulder. "Um, like, 'scuse me! Are you *supposed* to be up here?" The whiny voice matched what Layne saw when she turned her head back to answer the girl. She looked like she lived off seaweed and glitter, aggressive layers of makeup applied, and everything else that touched her body had a high-end designer label slapped on it.

"Piss off." Layne did not have time to deal with some nitwit thinking she could go on a power trip over a damn seating area.

The table right behind Layne where the girl had been seated was occupied by four other people. Two of the table occupants were nearly one entity by account of how close they were. The female was nearly mounted on the man's lap while heavily making out with him. She barely looked old enough to be legally allowed to drink. Her lengthy curls of black hair obscured the man's face all the while it looked like she was about to devour him whole.

The man's hands clutched the woman closer as she suggestively rubbed her body up against him. There was most definitely zero room for God between those two.

The other two individuals at the table were male and definitely out of their element in the club. They just looked stuffy and dressed like they were attending a business meeting instead of going out for a night full of debauchery.

"You can't be up here without a pass," the bratty voice interrupted Layne's observations.

Layne turned around to face the girl who looked like she would blow away with a strong gust of wind. "Oh? Gee, thanks. I will take that under consideration next time." Layne's words dripped with sarcasm.

You would have thought this chick would have gotten a clue that Layne didn't give a fuck and would have let it all go. But, no. She did not. She turned and looked at the two men who weren't engaged in the disgustingly aggressive display of affection, saying something to each of them.

While Layne couldn't hear over the loud lyrics of the music, she guessed it was something along the lines of 'She's being mean to me and I'm not getting my way, boo-hoo.' Layne shook her head in annoyance that anyone would be this territorial over the area around a damn table.

One of the men nudged the otherwise preoccupied man, not once but twice while relaying whatever was said to him by this broad. Finally, the preoccupied man peeled the woman off him enough to come up for air and investigate what was going on.

Layne had been ready to turn around and give up on locating the bathroom, but when she saw the man's face the second he pulled away from the maneater, Layne may as well have been knocked over the railing from the unsuspecting emotional assault.

How was it that Joey and she ended up at the same club in a city this big? It wasn't just her who was surprised by this, but it looked like he hadn't expected to see her here either. Oh, great.

Suddenly, the entire club felt incredibly tiny with the walls closing in on her. Layne's heart felt like shards of glass were stuck in it, and it took everything in her to not show any of this on her face. She had no right to be upset that he was moving on with some whore. That's right, now that girl was a whore who wasn't good enough for a guy Layne had ditched.

It wasn't clear when her feet started moving, but they did, and she just knew she needed to create distance between them. She rushed down the steps leading away from the VIP area down to where everybody else was gathered in the dance space.

Joey quickly shoved the girl off his lap as he slid out of the booth. "Layne, wait!"

She didn't even so much as look back behind her despite his call for her to hold up.

It might have been a few too many drinks that drove her brash reaction, but she eventually found the younger guy she had been dancing with a little bit ago. Like a good little Boy Scout, he had waited for her to return.

Layne snagged his hand, clutching onto it as she pulled him into the depths of the crowd on the dance floor. "Dance with me." The guy grinned, more than happy to oblige and yet so unsuspecting the motive behind her actions.

She pushed herself up against him, running her hands up the front of his torso and onto his chest while her body sensually moved to the rhythm of the music pulsing through the air. Layne spun around, pressing her ass right into his crotch and it was no surprise that this youngin' had a raging erection going on. She looked back over her shoulder at him with a smirk while she guided his hands down over her sides and the exposed flesh of her legs.

Joey hadn't given up on chasing her and was able to track her down even in this sea of people in a dark space with the strobe lights providing the only real means of lighting.

When he laid eyes on the guy dancing with Layne, his hands all over her, all he saw was red. Joey stepped up to them and gave a confrontational push to the guy. "Get your fuckin' hands off her!" He pulled Layne off to the side. "What the hell, Layne?"

"Don't touch me!" She shot him an icy glare.

The guy Joey shoved tried to intervene, "Look, man, she clearly doesn't want to talk to you." A-for-effort for the poor sap that was suddenly in the middle of this clusterfuck.

That sent Joey into a fury, he drew back and brutally punched the man in the face several times. Blood spattered from his mouth before he dropped to the ground, and now Joey's knuckles were smeared with the Boy Scout's blood.

Layne grabbed Joey by the arm and tugged with all her might. "Stop it! Jesus! What the hell is wrong with you?"

Joey turned to her. "You, Layne! You're what's wrong with me!" He was breathing heavily from the surge of anger that had just blown through his self-control.

She shook her head in disbelief that this was even happening. The two of them together were like absolute dynamite and C4 both going off in the same place at the same time.

"Leave me the hell alone!" She turned to leave the spot

there on the dance floor that had attracted some attention to the guy who had gotten on Joey's bad side just by existing.

"No, you don't." He grabbed her wrist to prevent her from running off again.

Layne spun around, her hand flying and slapping him right across his face. Instantly, she regretted it. The hurt that washed over Joey's face showed that he hadn't expected it either, his hand dropped her wrist, so she was free to go.

She left and pushed through the crowd, even though it wasn't even clear which way the exit was. Her mind was too fuzzy to recall where they had entered. Pushing past a few groups of people close to the outskirts of the crowd, she finally got eyes on the exit and was hell-bent on making it there.

CHAPTER TWENTY-EIGHT

Once Layne was outside and the bite of the cold air hit her skin, she was feeling confident she had left Joey behind. Oh, how wrong she was.

He called her name again. "Layne, stop!"

Fuck. She quickly walked down the street as fast as the heels on her feet would allow. He repeated her name a few more times, getting nearer. Then, finally, he rushed around in front of her to stop her unless she wanted to run right into him.

"Dammit, you don't just get to run off like this again."

Layne tried to side-step him only to be blocked again. "You don't get to tell me what to do!"

Realizing that they were apt to draw even more attention to themselves standing out in the open, Joey maneuvered her a few feet back into the alley off to the side from the sidewalk.

His hands gently landed on her arms trying to persuade her to stay there with him. "You completely ghost me with nothing but a vague note full of bullshit, and you expect that I'm not gonna have something to say about it?"

Layne tapped into the only thing she had to work with as a defense - her temper. Her hands gave a firm shove to his chest to get him away from her. "It was never meant to be more than just a fling, take a fucking hint!"

He allowed her to shove him, but he soaked in the force and remained right where he was. Stepping forward, this time he firmly pressed her back up against a brick wall so she didn't have room to push him away. The front of his body connected with hers.

"That's the biggest bunch of cockshit I've ever heard. You and I were both on the same page, then you just took off. I get things got messy and complicated, but you could have grown a pair and given us a chance to talk it over and work through it. Just tell me what changed." His eyes pleaded for her to be straight with him, and potentially herself.

Layne squirmed while being pinned up against that wall, disliking where this conversation was heading. While she was capable of defending herself, there was little she could do when he was using his strength to overpower her and his words to disarm her.

"Get your hands off me. It's over! Get over it! Go fuck your date in the club!" Her heart was leaping inside of her chest being so close to him, making her frantic to either escape or cave into the lustful feelings she had shoved down inside of her weeks ago.

"I was trying, Layne. I tried to get over it, and you don't get to judge me for that! You didn't give me a choice!" He verbally lashed back at her. He brought both his hands up to her face, holding it affectionately as he peered into her green eyes full of hurt. His thumb stroked across her cheek.

Joey pressed his forehead to hers while the rest of his body kept her pressed up against the side of the building in the dark alley. "You know I don't ask questions twice, Layney," his words softer now. "What has you running scared?"

She licked her lips in an effort to distract herself from the ache in her heart that was prompting her eyes to betray how she felt. Big, fat, salty tears were welling up. The way he called her Layney felt like home and all she wanted to do was run home, not away from it.

Swallowing hard she shifted her eyes to glance away from him, "I'm not sca—"

Joey put a tattooed finger against her mouth to stop her mid-response. "Look at me when you say it." He dropped his finger down away from the softness of her lips.

Pressing her lips together in a hard line, she looked back at Joey's face which was intimately close to her own. The scent of his cologne full of sage and sweet leather contaminated the air around her. Her lower lip faltered and trembled involuntarily as she got lost in his eyes.

There was a long pause as time seemed to stop between them both. When she finally spoke up, she couldn't say it any louder than a whisper. "Losing myself. Losing you." It was like sharing some deep dark secret she had never revealed to anyone else. Her biggest fear was giving all of herself to him only to have him torn away from her much like so many other times she had experienced in her life.

He took a moment to analyze her response before responding. "Never happening." Joey's mouth passionately claimed hers in a blindingly hot kiss.

It was then that Layne couldn't hold back anymore. She opened her mouth, welcoming his tongue to come intertwine with her own. Her hands went to the shirt he was wearing and slid up inside of it to feel the ripples of his abs straight up to the swell of his strong pec muscles on his chest. The familiar heat that he always made her feel between her legs was reignited with a demand to have every part of him.

He growled in excitement as Layne's hands made contact with his body, inciting him to claim her ass with his hands before dropping them down enough to lift her up. Joey forced her legs apart to wrap around his hips. The fabric of the dress gave away and rolled up to her waist, exposing the hot pink lace thong underneath.

His mouth pulled away from hers and moved down her neck towards the tops of her breasts on display above the daringly low neckline of her dress. His teeth bit into the fabric and tugged the dress down so her breasts popped free from their captivity. Joey's mouth took one of her stiff nipples hostage and assaulted it with his tongue.

She was already gasping for air as he worked over her nipples, his teeth nipping possessively at them. One of Layne's arms wrapped around the back of his neck for stability while the other dipped down between them to his belt. Her fingers unlatched it and yanked it open while she let out a light moan at the thought of what was already straining to get out of the front of his pants.

"My cock has been dying to fuck your sweet little pussy again, Layney. No amount of jerking off has helped how much the thought of you has had it aching." He gave another playful nip to the top of one of her breasts. His hand assisted in unbuttoning the top of his jeans and sliding the zipper down to allow his hardened length to spring out. "Are you going to scream for me like a good girl, hm?"

Layne now had both arms wrapped around his neck, one of her hands sliding up the back of his neck into the hair on the back of his head, gripping it hard. Her breathing grew more rapid out of eagerness.

She brought her mouth roughly back to his. Her teeth gave a bite and tug to his lower lip with a mischievous smile. "Only if you make me."

"Challenge accepted." His fingers pushed the thin strip of fabric away from her slick folds, and didn't hesitate to immediately sink his shaft into her. Layne gasped and then cried out in pleasure as she tilted her head back against the bricks behind her as her walls wrapped around him.

Joey let out a groan as he felt the tightness of her body welcoming him deep inside. Holding her up against the wall, he thrust his hips again this time with more force.

Layne's legs squeezed around his hips, moaning with each movement he made.

"That's right, Layney, you're doing such a good job of taking all of me. You're always so damn hot and ready for me to have you." He grunted as his pace began to pick up, letting feral instincts take over in pumping his cock in and out of her. There was no going easy after the high-strung emotions had played out between them. They both needed each other hard and fast.

After what felt like an eternity of them having been apart from one another, it was no surprise that an inferno of ecstasy was already intensifying at her core, nearly becoming unbearable. "Joey, yes, please. Don't stop!" It was becoming more and more challenging to get her words out now as all the lust and passion made her head delightfully light and foggy.

He possessively took her mouth with his once again out of need, like she was the last breath of fresh air on the planet. Afterward, his words were strained but demanding. "Beg me for it."

Her hips bucked against him, her body squirming as she neared the edge of absolute bliss. "Please." Her voice sounded so incredibly needy, even to her.

"Please, what?" He slowed his hips down to slow but intentional thrusts as he waited for her to respond.

"God, I want to cum all over you. Make me." Her body ached for him to push her over the edge while she locked her gaze on him.

"That's what I want to hear from my good girl," was all he said before he bucked his hips and pummeled himself back into her.

The tip of his length rammed into her at just the right spot deep inside her cunt over and over. Layne trembled and buried her face into the side of his neck as she gave out a long scream of absolute release.

Her warm arousal came all over his dick. As she

climaxed, Joey grunted and shuddered as he unloaded deep inside of her as he found his own peak. His hands dug into her thighs hard as he cursed while yelling out fiercely. "Ugh, fuck!"

While her face was still buried up against the side of his neck, Layne's body went limp around him as she tried to catch her frantic breaths.

Joey let out a sigh of contentment, lowering his lips to her throat and laying delicate little kisses on the skin there.

He whispered to her, "You will never lose me, and I will never let you lose yourself."

CHAPTER TWENTY-NINE

Layne had been working on trying to not let her insecurities and fears get the better of her when it came to Joey. Hard discussions were constantly on the table, and Joey had been there to talk her down when she felt like the world was against them. She was a realist, and in both of their lines of work, neither one of them was guaranteed a happy ending.

He had been a saint, giving her all the space to be the hot mess that she was known to be. In a twisted way, things almost resembled a sense of normalcy of an average life - almost. Most weeks they saw each other three or four times depending on their schedules.

She still sure as hell wasn't about to broach the topic with her dad about her love life. He would have a coronary if he ever found out about Joey. Maybe someday she would raise it, but she was still trying to deal with one difficult step at a time while keeping her father in the dark.

Liam had been keeping his distance, burying himself in

his work or a hooker - depending on the day. Layne considered that a win for everybody.

As far as anyone else knew, the skull-faced man who had been hired to eliminate Michael Franzetti from the playing board had moved on after the job was complete.

And today? Today was just another Tuesday, payday for the O'Reilly clan from all their clients.

Back at Slices of Heaven Pizzeria, the last stop on her collection route, Layne stood there counting a large sum of cash in her hands, "…forty-eight, forty-nine, five grand. I'm so proud of you, Kevin. You know how to count this week." She grinned at him as she tucked the wad of money into her bag. "If you keep this up, we may be able to start trusting you again."

Making quick work of this little check-in with Kevin to ensure he was keeping up with his payments to her family, she left to go back to her car. While sitting in the driver's seat, she texted Joey:

LAYNE

Working again tonight?

JOEY

Yeah, but it should be quick. In and out deal.

LAYNE

Good, because I have a job for you.

JOEY

If it involves burying my cock inside of you, I accept.

LAYNE

Show up by 9 or I'm starting without you.

JOEY
I'm never late.

A flurry of excitement settled deeply between her legs in anticipation of how this evening's plans were coming together. She dropped her phone into the cup holder of the center console and took off, heading uptown towards O'Reilly Manor to drop off the stack of cash in her possession from all the day's collections.

With an iced coffee in one hand and carrying a bag of cash in the other, she stepped inside her childhood home. Layne took another sip of the frigid brew, noting how unusually quiet it was inside the house. There was none of the typical hustle and bustle of workers coming and going and her father holding meeting after meeting.

She carried the bag upstairs into what was her old bedroom. She set her cup down on the Victorian-looking makeup vanity and entered the spacious walk-in closet where one of several safes in the house was located.

While spinning the dial on the safe she heard a voice break the silence. "I thought I heard someone come in."

Layne pulled open the safe's door after successfully unlocking it, she looked over and saw Mick standing there. "Hey." She smiled. "I was wondering where everybody was."

He stood there casually. "Your dad decided to take a trip up to Boston."

"Again? It's like the third time in the past two months." She glanced over at him with a perplexed look on her face that he had traveled north without saying a thing to her about it.

"Got me, you know how he is. No details until you need to know, and even then, it's the bare minimum." Mick shrugged, unbothered.

She unloaded the payments from the duffle into the safe one bundle at a time.

"Weekly collections go smoothly?" His hand motioned to all the money.

"Yeah. For once, everybody was on top of their shit." She grinned at him. Once the cold hard cash was all securely placed into the small vault, she locked things up.

Mick nodded. "That's good. We can't have people stepping out of line."

Layne approached the closet entrance where Mick's hulking form took up all the space. He stepped back, allowing her to get through the doorway back into the frilly pink bedroom.

Mere moments after passing him, she felt an iron grip yank her back by her shoulders and fling her into the wall roughly. Her body made contact with the unforgiving surface, and the force had her stumbling off to the side, her hands catching herself on a dresser.

Stunned, she looked over at Mick who had a look in his eyes she had never seen in all the years she knew him. She had heard stories of him from years ago, that he had been a violent and nearly psychotic force to be reckoned with, but she had never witnessed it first-hand. All she had ever known was the honorary uncle who had been full of nothing but support for her. "Mick, what the fuck?"

"Oh, Layne, you stupid little bitch." He stepped toward her, his words having disarmed her temporarily, she was slow to react when he grabbed for her. Barely ducking under his arm, she made a run for the door.

He was hot on her heels, and his hand latched onto her arm, giving a forceful tug as he spun her back around. The second the momentum spun her back to being face to face with him, the back of his massive hand made contact with her face. The impact sent her reeling down onto the floor with a thud.

The room was spinning as she lay there, willing it all to stop moving. Layne's watering eyes blurred her vision. Her heartbeat sounded louder than a fighter jet between her ears. It was unclear how long it was before she was rolled onto her back, looking up at the one person she never expected to betray her family like this.

Mick kneeled, his hand latched onto her throat and squeezed like a snake around its prey. Her fingers clawed at his grasp as stars began to prick at her consciousness. She yelled for help, but the words never came out.

"Don't fight it," he murmured to her.

She didn't have a lot to fight with, but she had enough. Her foot kicked against his chest with everything she had, which was enough to stagger him back after releasing his hold on her airway.

Layne rolled over with violent coughs wracking her body, pushed herself up onto her feet, and ran out of her bedroom. All the while, she was still fighting the wave of dizziness that was made worse by her movements.

Relying on basic survival instincts, she knew she had to

get out of there. Get out, Layne. Escape when death is the inevitable outcome of staying - just like her dad had always told her.

The thunderous footsteps were getting closer to her, or was that the pounding of the blood pumping furiously through her body?

Clutching onto the railing, she descended the main staircase clumsily. When she made it to the bottom step, she felt a force plow into her from behind sending her plummeting to the floor. A cry of surprise erupted from her mouth and echoed in the acoustics of the foyer. Still summoning every ounce of stubborn fight in her, she pushed up onto her hands.

Mick's hands yanked her up the rest of the way onto her feet by her upper arm and a fistful of her hair. The hold on her arm was so tight she swore it would take him very little to crush her bones. "Stay awhile, sweetheart, we're going to have a little chat." With his hand ensnared in her hair, he gave a harsh tug, causing her head to tilt back uncomfortably.

His eyes met her own, full of sinister motives and a cruel grin stretched across his mouth. Fuck.

CHAPTER THIRTY

She sat there in the dining room, ropes biting into her delicate wrists as they restrained her from moving from the chair. Her ankles were equally indisposed to the legs of the chair.

Layne glared over at Mick, the betrayal that she felt was pale in comparison to the amount of anger and seething that she had for the man. "All these years, and this was your plan? Why?" He had spent over thirty years working for her father, and now he was making a play for more power? She just couldn't comprehend it.

"Oh, Layne, sweetheart, you never were good at seeing the bigger picture." His hand that wasn't holding his gun lightly patted the top of her thigh.

"Enlighten me." She needed to keep this conversation going. Every minute he was talking to her was a minute more to try and find a way out of this seemingly hopeless situation.

He squatted down in front of her so they could look at each other on the same level. Mick shook his head, either really impressed with himself or disappointed in her.

"Because it's not just about me. Project 227 is my big break in this industry. I have been at your father's side for years, and the moment he knocked up your mother, he decided that instead of rewarding all my hard work and loyalty he would mindlessly pass the torch onto a clump of cells. All he could talk about was how proud he would be to hand off this business to blood. For all his touting about loyalty, being the pinnacle of this business, loyalty has meant nothing but shit to him."

Layne was in disbelief that all of this was because he was butthurt. Typical men. "Well, you know what they say about loyalty? Blood ties strengthen the roots of loyalty. I guess, you didn't have what it took."

Mick's face twisted with rage as he used the pistol in his hand to strike her across the face. Her head harshly turned with the impact. A cut on her cheekbone where the cold and unforgiving metal had connected. The broken skin cried a crimson trail down the side of her face, falling from the edge of her jaw onto her jean-clad leg.

"Always with the fuckin' mouth, Layne. I can't tell you how many times I've told myself that someone needed to give it a good hard smack." He chuckled, "But that wouldn't have taught you a lesson though, would it? You just can't help yourself."

He placed the muzzle of the gun on the seat of her chair between her legs, slowly inching it to her apex so it was pushed up against the crotch of her pants. "Just like you couldn't help yourself chasing dick all over the city." He partially rose and leaned in, his lips harshly rubbing against her ear as he whispered into her ear. "Just like your whore of a mother."

Layne's arms tensed with all the anger continuing to escalate inside of her, but unable to lash out without the freedom of her arms or legs. She pulled her head to the side to strain away from his sickening breath as far as she was able. His hand promptly latched onto her face, fingers harshly dug into her cheeks as he turned her to look right at him. His fingers smeared her own blood across her face as he did so. "You're going to learn a lot of brutal real-world lessons today, and I can't wait."

His grip finally relinquished its hold on her as he stepped back, licking the coppery flavor of her blood clean from his fingers. Afterwards, he retrieved a phone from his pocket, dialing a number. Placing it on speaker, Layne shifted uncomfortably in her seat not getting any reprieve from the tightly bound ropes.

Ring. Ring. Ring. Ri—

"Mick, what's going on?" Her heart sank, hearing her father's familiar voice at the end of the other line. She squeezed her eyes shut for a second already foreseeing where this was going. He was on a business trip up in Boston - hours away and Mick knew that was to his advantage.

"Oh, just a little restructuring of this organization." His eyes never left Layne even though she had no opportunity to go anywhere.

"What are you talking about?" Scott's voice was wary and impatient with the lack of clarity of Mick's response.

"I'm sick and fuckin' tired of being put below your spoiled brats. There's going to be a lot of changes around here after I'm done dealing with them."

There was a silence so thick on the other end from her father processing the gravity of the situation from words alone. After a few seconds, her father's cautious tone came across, "Where's your head at, Mickey?"

He smiled like he had been envisioning this moment for some time. "I have Layne here with me, why don't you ask her?"

"Layne? Layne, tell me what's going on." A slight tick of panic in his voice as he asked for her.

Her eyes locked on Mick's, she refused to give him the satisfaction of confirming she was even present.

"She's almost as stubborn as you are." Mick sounded impressed.

Without warning, he lifted the pistol and fired off a shot. It left her ears ringing at first but was quickly followed by a searing pain in her left shoulder that tore a scream from her mouth. "Ahh! Fuck!"

On the phone, a series of expletives were given by her father, though she didn't hear exactly what they were as the sudden onslaught of pain throbbed across the upper left area of her body. A wet warmth followed as her light blue shirt began to soak up the blood escaping the small hole that was now in her shoulder.

"I'm sorry, what was that, Layne?" Mick inquired with an evil smirk across his face.

"Go to hell! Gah!" She screamed out again as it seemed to help nominally with the pain.

Mick's voice was oozing with confidence now. "As I'm sure you can tell, Scotty, she's not feeling too hot right now. Here is what is going to occur if you want her to have a quick and painless death, because let's be straight with one another, she's not leaving here in anything but a body bag. Don't worry about missing out on this though, I will be sure to leave enough of her blood around the house, so you'll be cleaning it up for months."

"I trusted and confided in you. You were treated as part of my family, and this is how you repay me?" Her father was gritting his teeth through his words.

Mick sighed with exhaustion evident in his voice. "All talk. Where was all my glory in this?! You coddled your kids, promising them riches and power, and what did my family get? Your eternal gratitude and a pat on the back?"

Layne drew in harsh and deep breaths as she tried to control the sensation of pain wracking her body.

Mick continued, "A pat on the back is just not going to be good enough. I want the offshore accounts all under my control. Then, you're going to turn yourself in to Boston PD while you're up there and confess to every scheme you've ever been involved in. The Feds will come in and will lock your ass up and throw away the key for the past two years alone, while I pick up the fractured pieces of business operations here."

"The accounts will take time, Mick, you know that," Scott warned.

"I guess you will need to hurry and do what you can to

make them take less time. I already have people on the way to the Four Seasons Downtown to see to it that Liam is seen buckling under the pressure of the business, turning to a tragic encounter with a fatal dose of heroin. As for Layne, well, she and I will have to find a way to pass the time." The way he said the last few words made Layne's skin crawl and a wave of nausea rolled through her stomach.

"Son of a bi—"

Mick ended the call, cutting off her dad's words, and tossed the phone onto the table carelessly.

"You're a coward. You had to wait until my dad was out of town to make your move? You couldn't just face him directly like a man?" A sheen of sweat across her forehead from the nagging pain embedded in her shoulder. Her body involuntarily shook from a combination of adrenaline, anger, and agony.

His laughter abruptly burst out of him. "I'm ten times more of a man than your dad has ever been. Maybe I will show you before our time here is up." He walked behind her, a hand gripping onto her injured shoulder.

Layne writhed as the deep ache flipped back into an intense shooting pain. Biting her lower lip, she tried not to cry out.

"Don't hold back on my account." He gave her shoulder another squeeze. "I won't mind hearing you scream."

Things went dark.

For a moment even Layne wasn't sure if she had blacked out or not, but she blinked her eyes a few times and realized it was just the lights that cut out in the house.

Mick released her shoulder, and she could hear his footsteps as he moved away from her, murmuring to himself. "Damnit."

She tried to will her eyes to adjust quicker to the dark, but it wasn't happening fast enough. Her hands furiously tugged and pulled against the ropes holding her there to the chair. The burn of the ropes rubbing against her skin was nothing by comparison to what would happen if she didn't get free.

That's when she heard a thud come from the room above her. Instinctively, she looked up, wondering if she truly had heard anything at all or if it had been her imagination, or possibly delirium. While her heart continued pounding in her body, she continued to fight against her restraints.

Mick's footsteps were coming closer to her once more, she could feel his presence through the shadows. He stopped short, and suddenly all Layne heard were the sounds of two men grunting and Mick's strangled voice. The movement of air wisped around her, indicating there was a hell of a struggle going on.

The sound of a high-pitched shot pierced through the air. Layne flinched. No new pain that she could feel was reassuring that she hadn't been injured again.

A large thump occurred next to her, the thump of a lifeless body. Whose body? She couldn't be sure.

Hands settled on top of hers as the outline of a body appeared before her.

"Stop moving." The masculinity dripping from the voice in front of her was unmistakable.

She froze in her seat. "Joey?" Her voice broke with a sudden surge of relief.

The lights came flickering back on, and before her, he had a knife in hand that sliced through the ropes with ease. He was crouched in front of her, wearing his typical all-black ensemble except the infamous mask he normally wore while doing his dirty work was missing.

She leaped up from her seat, tossing her arms around his neck and immediately regretting it as her left shoulder protested, causing her to whimper. "How did you know I was in trouble?"

He frowned as he pulled back and inspected the blood-saturated shirt she was wearing and the marks on her face and throat. Anger flashed across his face at how extensively Mick had injured her. If Joey could have resurrected and killed the bastard again, he would have taken his time. "Your father's men up in Boston contacted me. I have some friends on the way to Liam right now."

She found herself stunned that he managed to coordinate all of this on a dime. When she looked down at the floor, she saw Mick's body lying face-down with a puddle of blood around his head that was gradually growing larger with each passing second.

Joey spoke in a hurry. "I only have a few minutes, let's get you outside."

"A few minutes for what?" Her attention was drawn back to him.

"You're hurt, Layne, you need to get checked out. C'mon." Stepping around the fresh corpse in the dining room, he led her outside with a supportive arm around her waist.

As her emotions began to come down from their heightened state, the blood that soaked into her shirt no longer felt warm but cool and tacky. Her head was beginning to float from the lack of adrenaline keeping her from succumbing to the unfortunate side effects of being shot.

Joey recognized the paleness in her face and coaxed her to sit down on the front stoop. "Hey, hang in there. Sit." Always giving orders this one.

She didn't have the strength in her to argue. Instead, she did as he ordered, and she plunked her ass down on the cold brick step. Her hand held onto her wounded shoulder, unclear if the pressure made it feel better or worse.

"I will be back." He took off back into the house, for what she wasn't sure but before she could ask questions he was already gone.

That's when the lights captured her attention, the reds and blues speeding down the street. Sirens wailed in the air. Once an entire herd of police cars were in front of the house, everything became a blur.

The city's finest immediately ushered her away from the house, asking her a series of questions until the paramedics arrived on the scene. She half paid attention to the flurry of activity around her, wondering if Joey was still inside the house.

As she sat on the back bumper of the ambulance, refusing to sit on a gurney like a wounded animal, one paramedic asked about her medical history while the other inspected her shoulder. Her head was thoroughly throbbing from the headache that had begun to take over. After medical personnel convinced her she needed to go to Mount Sinai, she began to climb into the back of the ambulance with the assistance of the medics.

Something caught her eye though, causing her to pause mid-step.

It was hard to tell from her limited view, but a man who looked like Joey was standing across the street, talking to one of the officers. They grasped hands and pulled each other in for a hug, with Joey patting the cop on the back with a smile. Everything about the encounter appeared friendly, like they were long-time buddies just shooting the shit.

"Ma'am? We need to get you to the hospital." The sound of the female paramedic's voice interrupted her thoughts. She blinked a few times, conflicted with what she thought she was witnessing.

The paramedic spoke again, "Ma'am? We really have—"

"I know." Layne's words were impolitely short with the woman.

Up into the back of the ambulance Layne went, where she was transported to the hospital only a few miles away. Her thoughts nagged her as she over-analyzed everything in her head during the ride.

When she arrived at the hospital, she disconnected emotionally from the situation trying to clear her head of anything at all. A series of tests were run, imaging was taken, and so many questions were asked.

As it turns out, Layne had gotten lucky that the bullet

had missed a series of arteries, nerves, and bones and only damaged her flesh as it passed through. It physically didn't feel lucky at the moment, but things were looking up when they began pumping painkillers in through her IV.

Feeling the tug of a drug-induced slumber on the horizon, Layne laid her head back on the uncomfortably shallow hospital pillow and let the meds pull her under.

CHAPTER THIRTY-ONE

Having been released from the hospital nearly ten days ago, Layne was still in recovery mode. The doctors sent her home with a series of medications and orders for physical therapy to restore full use of her left arm.

A bouquet of fresh flowers was neatly placed in a vase on her kitchen table. They were a simple and beautiful arrangement of white roses mixed with the rich purples of delphiniums, providing a light yet pleasant scent to the room. The get-well gift had been delivered without a name on the card, though she had her suspicions about who the sender was.

Joey had been M.I.A. since the entire ordeal with Mick leaving her even more cranky than her shoulder was already making her. Her thoughts about what she thought she had seen before getting into the ambulance had consumed her, and now with him being radio silent, she couldn't quiet her mind about it. She desperately wanted to be angry with him, but that was the thing about her relationship with Joey, she had problems standing and maintaining her ground. He was her Achilles' Heel, and she was his.

After speaking with the police, she learned that the house lights had been cut remotely through a phone app. Layne hadn't always been appreciative of new technology, but in this case, she was grateful. The cops had received an anonymous phone call reporting suspicious activity and shots fired at her father's residence which is what made for the swift arrival of the boys in blue. As for their investigation? It was an open and shut case based on Layne's recollection of events, sans Joey, and perhaps a little monetary incentive to those on the take thanks to the Scott O'Reilly bribery fund.

Liam had been railing his so-called date at the Four Seasons when a small crew of skull-masked men busted down the door of his suite. The men dragged her brother to a temporary safehouse, barely allowing him to collect his pants on the way out. Whether or not the crew had spooked Mick's hitman or if it had been a bluff all along wasn't known.

As for Scott O'Reilly? He hauled ass back from Boston and immediately sorted through the ranks to weed out any potential sympathizers of Mick's plight. It had been an ugly and violent process, but it sent a message loud and clear: no one is safe if you fuck with his family. As head of the organization, he set forth a new campaign to solidify his foothold in the city. With Franzetti's faction crumbling without their fearless leader, he was able to salvage a few good little soldiers and left the rest to their own devices.

The Flannigan family held a small funeral for Mick, in which her dad was in attendance. Despite the pisspoor ending to Mick's story, it still had been a lifelong friendship and Layne was sure that deep down her father had to mourn the tragedy in his own way.

Rebecca had summoned her natural inner caretaker, bringing Layne a series of homemade foods to help stock up a freezer stash. Layne was confident that she would never have to order takeout, like, ever again. Amongst the variety of foods, there was a particularly delicious-looking turkey tetrazzini she was looking forward to digging into tonight. In addition to all the meal prep, her bestie had left her very strict instructions pinned to the fridge:

1. GET REST.
2. SERIOUSLY. SEE #1 ABOVE.
3. DO YOUR PHYSICAL THERAPY.
4. EAT SOMETHING.
5. HYDRATE.
6. BINGE-WATCH TRASHY TV.
7. CALL ME ASAP IF YOU NEED ANYTHING.
XOXO, REBECCA

Layne had done her best to abide by the rules set forth for her, but listening to directions wasn't her strong suit. To make sure Layne didn't completely disregard her, Rebecca insisted on coming over for a taco night tomorrow.

After the ding of the microwave chimed, Layne

grabbed the corner of the steamy hot bag of popcorn and brought it into the living room. The distinct aroma of the buttery snack filled the air as she took her seat on her sofa. She used her teeth to tug on one corner while pulling the other with her right hand to pry open the bag. Setting the bag in her lap, she grabbed the remote on the cushion next to her and un-paused an episode of *You*.

"Man, that guy is a freak." A husky voice that made her legs weak commented from behind her. Knocking her popcorn off her lap onto the floor, she spun around in her seat to look back at Joey. Layne's first instinct was to greet him with a smile, and she struggled to prevent it from tugging at her lips when she saw him standing there behind her couch.

"Says the guy who has made a habit of having never *not* broken into my house." She picked up a kernel of popcorn off the sofa and flicked it at him.

"If you want, I can go back outside and ring the door-bell if it would make you feel better." He had a smartass smirk on his face, but instead of making good on that offer, he leaned over onto the back of the couch on his forearms, a warm sparkle in his puppy dog brown eyes.

She turned back around in her seat doing her best to ignore the charm he was trying to pour on just by giving her that look. "So, what are you doing here?"

"Figured you could use some company." He spoke like he hadn't been invisible for the last week and a half.

"I could have used company the night I got shot." She fired right back at him casually.

He audibly sighed behind her, not with annoyance but with the knowledge that he had some damage control to do here. Layne kept her eyes focused on the television, but her brain wasn't focused enough to retain what was happening onscreen.

"Look, I know I haven't been around. I couldn't be." Kudos to him for sounding decently apologetic.

"Oh?" Not hiding the disinterest in her voice.

"Layne, don't be like that." He begged her.

"Like what?" Feigning ignorance at what he was possibly referring to.

"You know what. I get it, you're pissed, and you have every right to be."

She rose from the couch and walked over to a drawer on the far side of her coffee table. Using her uninjured arm, she pulled it open and retrieved a manilla folder with some papers in it. Going around the back of the couch, she shoved the file into his hands.

Joey took the folder, opened it up, and flipped through a few pages. His face fell at what was inside. Sheet after sheet of information on the very thing he had been avoiding telling her. Documents reflecting his assistance in police investigations as an informant.

"*Pissed*? I don't think that even begins to describe what I felt when my guy brought this to my attention. I saw you that night, acting like you and that cop were best bros. From there, I started to piece it all together. I had hoped I was wrong, Joey, I really did. You knew things about the 227 project that Franzetti didn't even know. The way you acted when we encountered those two officers in the subway. Not to mention all the other things I ignored because I have been so stupidly blinded by you."

"Layne," he reached out to touch her arm.

She pulled back from him. "Don't." She stared at him, searching for a sign of who he really was underneath the façade he put up. "How long have you been feeding information to the cops? The entire time I've known you?"

He stood there silently, confirming her assumption.

Layne scoffed at how she had been so blind to it all. "What about me? How much have you told them?" She was starting to downward spiral at all the things that could have been shared about her professional or even personal life.

He stepped up to her, his hands holding onto her face as he pressed his forehead to hers. "No, you stop right there. The only things I shared about you were irrelevant and only related to other cases. They've got nothing on you, I kept everything about you to myself."

Her eyes gazed up into his. "Liam? My dad?"

"Some stuff, but nothing solid they can stand on." He spoke like it was all no big deal.

"God, I trusted you! My dad trusted you!" Her temper rearing its vicious head. She pulled her face back from his hands, and he let her as his hands fell back down to his sides.

"Layney, I didn't have any other choice." His words were supposed to be reassuring, but they did little to settle Layne down.

Not to mention, his using her nickname suddenly did

little to calm her. "Don't 'Layney' me, that's bullshit. There is always another choice!"

He ran his fingers through his sandy-colored hair in desperation, trying to find a way to make things right with her. She walked over to her front door and flung it open. "Leave." When he didn't immediately walk out the door she raised her voice. "Get out!"

A look of defeat washed over his face as he joined her at the front door. "I'm so sorry." He leaned in to give her one of the most tender kisses she had ever felt from him. It was full of bittersweet affection, and every fiber of her being was screaming at her to cave into the delicious addiction that he was.

It bordered on painful to pull her mouth back from his. "If I ever see you again, I will fucking shoot you myself. Get out and stay out." She averted her eyes from him as she waited for him to get the hell out of her home.

He backed away from her and took his sullen leave. Layne didn't hesitate to slam the door shut behind him. She pressed her back against the closed door and looked up at the ceiling trying to process the whirlwind of emotions flooding her body.

Layne pushed away from the door and screamed out in frustration, her hands swiping her purse and today's mail off the table in the foyer. Her purse's contents spilled out across the floor, scattering in various directions. Her hot tears relentlessly rolled down her cheeks at his betrayal, at seeing him leave, at him never knowing what else was going on behind the curtain.

She slid down to the floor onto her knees, sobs being

choked out while she picked up the mess she created one item at a time. Her hands trembled as she pulled the last item up off the floor. Layne stared at the lab and biopsy results that one of her associates was able to hack from the hospital system before crumpling them up in her hand.

Life was going to get a hell of a lot messier.

EPILOGUE

Six months later

I t seemed cruel that this was taking place on such a beautiful day, full of sunshine that beat down on the perfectly manicured lawn that seemed to expand off into the distance forever.

Headstones of various sizes and colors were planted every few feet around them. The vibrant colors of the flowers cluttering the ground in front of them were far too cheerful to be considered appropriate. The birds in the sky were even singing their cheerful songs without regard. All of it just seemed wrong. Today should have been as dark as her thoughts were.

Layne stood there, falling victim to the storm of her thoughts instead of listening to the priest standing over the gleaming red oak casket. A sea of people with tissues in their hands stood around the open plot. She wondered how many of them truly cared, and how many simply came to solicit some juicy gossip.

Being here was all about putting on a brave face and all that political bullshit. She felt nothing but fury and chaos deep within her soul. She wanted to cave to the darkness spreading throughout her. She was regretting every choice that led up to this point, right down to the shoes she had chosen this morning.

When she looked up once more, all the attendees were slowly dispersing to return to their vehicles. Murmurs of condolences spoken to her as they passed by.

If she never heard another "I'm sorry" in her lifetime, it still would be one too many. Each expression of sympathy added fuel to the fiery anger being pent up inside of her.

Her legs felt stiff from standing still for such a lengthy amount of time, the bottoms of her feet pleading for relief from the heels she had chosen, and all the muscles along the back of her spine up to the back of her head in knots from the tension in her body. Her eyes were dry and tired. Layne's jaw ached from being clenched so that she didn't unleash the venom she wanted to spew.

Time passed slowly while she stood there, and yet before she knew it, everyone had left to return to their regularly scheduled lives. Layne felt a hand rest on her lower back as a voice spoke to her the way you would speak to a predator who could strike to kill at any sudden sight or sound.

"There was nothing you could have done. You have to know that." He assured her.

She didn't buy that. "There was everything that I could have done."

"Let him go. He'd want that."

She squeezed her eyes shut again, finding darkness behind her closed lids.

Silently, she made a vow at that moment that things were going to change.

To be continued in **Layne Closure Ahead**.

ACKNOWLEDGMENTS

To my husband: I love you forever and always. You've always pushed me to work towards my dreams, and here I am, able to make it a reality. I could have never done this without you being my rock. Bonnie & Clyde Forever.

To my son: You are too young to even recognize this achievement, but Mama loves you more than the stars and the moon, and you are the motivation keeping me going on this exciting journey. Always chase your dreams, they don't have an expiration date.

To my Good Little Sluts: Without your guidance and support in taking a baby author under your wings, I would have never made it this far. So thank you from the bottom of my heart for all the advice, laughter, and soundboarding. Also, thank you for making sure I didn't have a breakdown.

To my PA, Cheryl: You have been my cheerleader and giver of tough love. You believed in me even when I was struggling to believe in myself. Thank you for helping me spread the word about my baby book. I would have been lost without you!

To all my alpha/beta/ARC readers: Thank you for taking a chance on a brand new author and being part of this amazing journey. Without all your input and feedback, this story would not be nearly the same.

Cover by Author Maree Rose: I bow down before you for this amazing creation that exceeded my wildest dreams!

Editing by Baldwin Editing Services: Thank you for putting up with my craziness, answering my questions, and for the comma trauma!

About the Author Photography Credit to Pryceless Moments Photography: Thank you for making this mama feel good about rocking her new and crazy adventure!

Special mention to Jen who caught this gem:

"ONE OF THE MEN SLAMMED A **FISH** INTO JOEY'S STOMACH IN AN EFFORT TO SUBDUE HIM, CAUSING HIM TO DOUBLE OVER."

Thank you for making sure that Joey was not assaulted by a tuna during the making of this novel.

Sadie Winchester is a romance author residing in the Pine Barrens of New Jersey with her husband, her son, and their two cats (Thor & Loki). She began her love for writing in high school, drafting stories on a popular internet platform.

The dream of writing and publishing a full-length novel first manifested a couple of years after she married the love of her life. However, it took a back burner as she focused on other adventures and goals. Finally, after becoming a mother and finding a way to rediscover herself, she was inspired by another new author to commit to this long-term dream.

When Sadie is not writing up her stories or getting lost in books, she is spending time with her family. She enjoys working out, cooking, visiting microbreweries, and binge-watching *Supernatural*.

You can connect with Sadie in the following ways:
SadieWinchester.com or Linktr.ee/SadieWinchester

amazon.com/author/sadiewinchester

facebook.com/sadiewinchesterauthor

goodreads.com/sadiewinchester

instagram.com/sadiewinchesterauthor

tiktok.com/@sadiewinchesterofficial

bookbub.com/profile/sadie-winchester

www.ingramcontent.com/pod-product-compliance
Lightning Source LLC
Chambersburg PA
CBHW070520310726
48976CB00002BA/492